YING YANG

YING YANG

IMITATION & GENOCIDE

BOOK 2

IN LOVING MEMORY

LEROY WEEDEN SR

1922 – 2005

To order additional copies of this book, contact:
Enchantment Line Productions
www.enchantmentlineproductions.com
www.yingyang1.com
customerservice@yingyang1.com

TABLE OF CONTENTS:

Introduction..7

Chapter 1: Vacation................................8

Chapter 2: Pieces Of The Puzzle........................12

Chapter 3: The Power Of Imitation......................18

Chapter 4: Destruction...............................23

Chapter 5: The Battle Begins........................30

Chapter 6: The Broken Hearted......................39

Chapter 7: A Woman Scorned........................49

Chapter 8: Disasters Unfold..........................61

Chapter 9: The Plan Unfolds..........................74

Chapter 10: The Beginning Of The End.................85

Chapter 11: Man Vs. Woman.........................95

Chapter 12: Crystal's Past............................99

Chapter 13: A Test Of Strength......................108

Chapter 14: Time Struggle...........................115

Chapter 15: Crystal Vs. Everyone....................123

Chapter 16: Forgiven................................130

Chapter 17: War On Ying Yang......................139

Chapter 18: Darkside Vs. Frost......................149

Chapter 19: Rise Of Evil.............................156

INTRODUCTION

Darkside was hanging from the top of the Seattle Space Needle, seemingly lifeless. Chaos was down on the ground, face-down. Trinity and her brother were nowhere to be seen. As it was, death was in the air from the carnage that had befallen them and it seemed all hope was lost...

CHAPTER 1:

VACATION

It had been ten months since Darkside and his friends had defeated Phobos. Darkside was away on vacation on his home planet and had taken April with him. Trinity, her brother, and Chaos all stayed back on Earth. Like usual, they were all hanging out. Trinity was feeling the same disappointment whenever Darkside would not take her out. Trinity looked at her brother and said to him, "I can't believe he went home and took her with him."

Her brother replied to her, "He just doesn't look at you that way. Maybe you should just give it up." To this, Trinity scoffed and rolled her eyes. Meanwhile, back home on the planet Ying Yang Darkside was showing April around. As they were walking the streets, he ran into some old friends that he had known for a while.

Darkside called out, "Ojohna!"

He replied in cheer, "Hey Darkside, I haven't seen you in a long time!"

Darkside and April walked over to them. "This is April." He said, "April this is Ojohna and Dosha."

Ojohna said, "It's been so long since we've seen you!"

Darkside replied, "Yeah it's been quite some time!"

Dosha asked Darkside "Is this your mate?"

Darkside said, "No, this is my good friend."

April had said hello, and April said, "Oh, you're hanging out with your granddaughter!"

Ojohna and Dosha looked at each other and then at April. Darkside cut in and said, "No, that's not his granddaughter! That's his mate." April had a look of confusion on her face. Darkside then said, "It's a long story. I'll tell you later."

Ojohna said, "Well it was really great seeing you Darkside but we've gotta move out. Lots to do today."

"Great seeing you guys too!" Darkside said. "Take care!"

As April and Darkside continued walking, April said, "Wow this place looks like home… but it's not home."

Darkside said, "It was the same for us when we came to Earth."

"I can't get wait to get back and tell everybody about it." April said.

Darkside asked, "Who are you gonna tell?"

She replied, "Oh, just my sister. She's off in Egypt seeing the pyramids but I can tell her I went to a whole other universe!"

Back on Earth, in what seemed to be an abandoned warehouse just outside of Albuquerque, New Mexico, Stan Jones had a little laboratory that he had built up. He was there with his assistant Mark. Stan had said, "Are you excited, Mark? Tomorrow is the big day."

"I am but I'm a little nervous." Mark replied.

"There's no reason to be nervous." Stan said. "Everything will work out great."

A week had went by. Darkside and April were on their way back to Earth. Trinity and the others expressed excitement for their return and she thought to herself, "I bet she tried to put the moves on him while they were gone. I knew I should have went with them."

Soon enough, they had arrived home. Chaos asked, "How was the trip? And home? How is everybody?"

Darkside, "It's good! I even saw the judge that kicked me off. He asked about you. He asked if you would ever return home. I told him that I wouldn't be coming back but I couldn't speak for you."

Chaos replied and said, "Yeah I don't think I'd go back either. I like it here. We all do." He then asked April, "So what did you think of our home planet?"

She replied, "It was very nice! A lot of it reminded me of here! It was just a little different because people from other planets visit Ying Yang and it's not here, with the exception of you guys coming here."

Chaos said, "Yep, it is different. A lot of similarities but there are a lot of differences between the two planets."

She said, "I can't wait until my sister gets back. She's the only other person that knows about you guys. I can't wait to tell her that I went to a whole different planet!"

While the group was rejoicing, in south Egypt April's sister Jasmine was on a tour of the pyramids. As they were leaving, there was a construction site and while walking by the tour guide gave facts about the pyramids. They passed directly by the construction area. The ground have gave way and Jasmine and three other had fallen down into the hole. The tour guide said, "Nobody panic! We'll get somebody to get you two out!"

As Jasmine sat up she moved her hand and felt something hard in the ground. She brushed away the sand. It was a little box. She picked up the very small box and looked at it in utter curiosity. There were guards on the way to the hole they had fallen into on the construction site. She immediately placed the box into her purse to conceal it.

The guards helped her and the others up to the top surface and they continued the tour. Soon enough the vacation was over and she was heading back home to see her sister.

CHAPTER 2:

PIECES OF THE PUZZLE

April was at the airport waiting for her sister's flight to arrive. Chaos was there with her, and was genuinely excited to meet April's sister. He was the only one out of the group who had met her prior to today. The flight arrived and they picked her up.

The two sisters ran to each other and wrapped their arms around one another and April asked, "How was the trip to Egypt?"

"It was pretty good!" Jasmine said. "Very historical. I had a bit of an accident though. I fell into a hole at a construction site, but I found this box.

April asked, "A box?"

"Yeah. There was this small box." Jasmine said.

April said, "A small box…"

"Yeah! I'll show it to you!" Jasmine exclaimed. She pulled the box out of her purse and handed it to April. April looked at it.

"Wow…" She said. "All these tiny markings on it. Ancient! Chaos have you ever seen anything like this?"

He reached out and picked up the box. "No," Chaos said, "I have never seen anything like this. Out of all the planets I've went to I have never seen markings like these."

He gave the box back to Jasmine. "Yeah I never saw anything like it before. It makes a really awesome souvenir. Not like the other tourists. They bought hats and shirts and dumb things like that."

Her sister simply laughed. "Well at least you didn't settle for a boring souvenir for your vacation."

As Jasmine went to put the box back into her purse she accidentally dropped it. She had tried to catch it when she fumbled it but it hit the ground and broke into seven pieces. "My souvenir!!!" Jasmine shrieked in despair.

As she bent over to pick up the pieces, the seven pieces scattered in all different directions. April said, "What the…!?" Many of the pieces flew out of the airport as if attracted by a magnet, attracting looks of confusion from other people in the airport. April then said, "I think it's time to go!"

As the three of them quickly left the airport to head back to April's place, Chaos had commented in the car, "That was odd! That box, when it broke, the pieces took off on their own!"

Jasmine said, "That was pretty weird! It's something bad, I'm sure."

"Well it's nothing that Chaos and his brother can't handle, right?" April asked.

Chaos said, "If anything happens, trust me. We'll take care of it."

The pieces from the box were in the air flying different directions while this group continued their trip to April's place. There was a man walking down the street. One of the pieces came and hit him in the back of the head. The man turned around and didn't see anybody. The piece that had hit him in the back of the head had integrated into his skull. There was a woman sitting outside of a café in France having coffee with her friend. A piece flew and hit her in the back of the head and just as she turned to look, it bonded with her head as well. There was another man in New York City getting out of his car to go to work and another piece hit him in the back of the head as well and when he turned to see what it was, it too integrated with his head. A woman just outside in her front yard in a small town in Georgia had a piece of the box fly to her and it merged with her head just as the others did. Downtown Chicago, there were two men and a woman all sitting outside at a pizza parlor having lunch. And a piece hit all three each in the back of their heads, fusing to their heads just like the other integrated pieces of the box with their hosts.

Meanwhile, back in the abandoned warehouse in Albuquerque, Stan Jones was standing in front of a chamber. Lights were flashing and smoke filled the chamber. An evil, sadistic smile spread over Stan's face. Suddenly the flashing lights stopped and a dead silence overcame the room. Stan stood in front of the open door to the chamber. Peering into the chamber the smile grew even wider. He said, "This time nobody will stop us!"

Back at April's place all six of them were gathered around in the living room. Chaos said to Darkside, "I was thinking about going to train this weekend. You should go too, brother. The others are coming, join us!"

Darkside replied, "Naw I don't think so. I'm just going to stay here. Not like we have to go anywhere. Trinity and her brother get funding from the government for being superheroes. You go. The only things I need are a nap, nap, dinner, and another nap."

Chaos said to his brother, "You need to be more productive! It's like you're wasting your life. There's so much more you can do."

He replied, "I'm not wasting time! I'm making sure I'm well rested in case something happens! The way I look at it, I'm training very well!"

Jasmine cut in and said, "I wish I could be lazy all the time. I gotta go back to work tomorrow. The vacation is over for me."

Darkside laughed and said, "I was thinking about taking a vacation."

Trinity then said, "A vacation? You don't do anything but sleep!"

Darkside chuckled. "I told you I work all the time. They're called power naps."

Trinity rolled her eyes and looked away. April said, "I know you've got to be excited, sis. You move into your new place on Monday!"

Jasmine replied, "I know! I can't wait! It'll be nice not having a roommate anymore."

Meanwhile in Georgia, there was a husband and wife who were fighting. The man yelled at his wife saying, "You need to do something. We have bills and you need to work! Times are hard!"

She replied to her husband, "I wanna work but I can't! You know I've been hurt ever since the car accident!"

He replied saying, "I know you had the accident a couple of years ago but it doesn't make you incapable of working! Bills are piling up and they cut my hours at work. You have to try to find a job. I can't support all three of us on the money that I'm making now!"

The woman yelled out to her husband, "You just don't understand."

"Oh I understand…" He said. "You're just being selfish. You don't wanna help your family!"

"It's not like that! I do want to help but I can't!" She said.

"You're just being a lazy bitch!" He yelled.

She looked at her husband and said, "No. I'm too hurt to work. You just don't understand. I don't have to take this. I'm going to my friend's house for the night." As she approached the door to leave, she said, "I'm not being lazy." And as she reached to open the door she fell over in pain.

Her husband said, "Oh great. Now you're going to fake like you're hurt!"

"I'm not faking it! My head hurts! It feels like my head's about to explode!"

A small piece of metal fell out of the back of her head. She cried out, "What's that!?" The piece of metal was coated in her blood. However, at the back of her head there was no blood. Soon the pain disappeared and she stood up.

The husband said, "What's going on?"

She replied, "I don't know." The piece of metal rose from the ground as it dripped with her blood. The piece of metal flew straight through the closed door putting a hole through it, and then flew into the sky. She ran into her husband's arms crying in fear screaming. "What's going on???"

"I don't know." He said as he held her. "…I have no idea."

CHAPTER 3:

THE POWER OF IMITATION

Stan Jones was driving a white van with no windows. He had just arrived in Phoenix, Arizona. He drove up to the front of City Hall and got out of the van after stopping it. He walked around the back of the van with a megaphone in his left hand. He lifted the megaphone and said, "Good afternoon, ladies and gentlemen! Allow me to introduce myself! I am Stan Jones!" The people turned and looked at him.

"As some of you may know or have read about a year ago in New Mexico with the Fear Monster and how the great Michael Smith saved the day, I'm here to tell you that I was the mastermind behind the monster. This time, I've done things differently. I have a new creation! It will lead the way as I conquer this world, so all of you get ready for the Stan Jones era!"

There was a man across the street who yelled, "Who the hell are you? Why should we listen to you?"

Stan Jones then said, "That's a very good question… Why should YOU listen to ME… Very good question indeed…"

"I'm not listening to you and nobody else here is gonna listen to you." The man across the street yelled.

"Well I know nobody wants to listen to me, but you're going to. Allow me to introduce my greatest creation." Stan yelled

As he stepped away from the back of the van, the back doors of the van blew off. Everyone stared in shocked silence. There was a man who stepped out of the back of the van. He was covered up, most of his face was completely obscured. Stan announced into the megaphone, "This man here is the reason you will all bow to Stan Jones!"

The man across the street said, "Some guy dressed like the Grim Reaper is gonna enslave us? I should walk across the street and beat you myself!"

Stan yelled out to the man, "Bring it!!!"

The man approached Stan. Just as he stepped right in front of the mad scientist, a smirk crept across Stan's face and he began to laugh. The man asked, "You think this is funny? I'm about to bash your face in!"

The covered-up man walked over to the two of them. He grabbed the pedestrian by the arm. He yelled out in pain, and Stan laughed in excitement. Stan told the monster, "Let him go." The monster released the man as he cried in agony. Stan looked down at the man and said, "I want you to kneel before me and kiss my boot."

As the pedestrian clutched his arm with tears rolling down his face, Stan yelled at him again, "Kiss my boot!!!"

The man leaned down and kissed Stan's boot. Stan said, "That's a good boy. Now go and tell everybody you see that Stan Jones in in charge!"

The man got up and ran as fast as he could and as far as he could. Stan said, "Well it's time to get to business!" His eye caught a lady off to the side. "I see you on your cell phone! I bet you're trying to call the cops."

The woman replied, "No! I-I wasn't going to all the cops!"

Stan laughed. "Don't play dumb with me, bitch. Call the cops! I want you to! Tell them that Stan Jones is here. The same guy that went to New Mexico with the Fear monster. Tell them to send everybody!

Before long a helicopter was above them, filming what was taking place. They shined a spotlight on Stan and the monster. Stan then announced into the megaphone, "Thank you! This is how it should be! The spotlight on Stan Jones! Now, I'm gonna do a demonstration of why you fools should obey me!"

He looked over at the monster and said, "Show these fools just what we are capable of."

The monster walked around right in front of Stan, reached out with his hand and grabbed Stan by the neck. Stan could barely breathe. The monster then said, "No. I'm not listening to you. For years I've listened to you. You were right, Stan. All these years of being your assistant have taught me one thing: I'm really sick and tired of listening to people like you whine and complain. But you did teach me one thing good. From this point on, I will be nobody's assistant. The world will be MINE."

While Stan gasped for air, the monster maximized its grip and crushed Stan's entire neck. He released his grip and Stan's corpse dropped to the ground. He turned around and looked at the people watching him and said, "Listen up, you fools! Forget about what Stan said. I'm in charge now!" He slowly lifted up and took off his hood and he looked identical to Darkside.

Meanwhile, there was a man who was at home crying. His friend walked in and said, "Steve, you need to pull it together!"

Steve replied, "It's just so hard! I miss her!"

His friend replied, "I know. You're letting yourself fall apart! Look at you, man. You look like a mess! Just how much junk food are you gonna eat?"

As Steve continued crying he said, "Just a little bit more…" And continued stuffing his face.

"There's no reason to be punishing yourself this way. She wasn't worth it." His friend said. "You can do so much better."

Steve cried out, "No! I need her!" And then continued to stuff his mouth with fistfuls of chocolate cake. Suddenly, Steve cried out in agonizing pain.

"What's going on?" His friend yelled.

"I don't know!" Steve yelled. "I feel like my head is about to explode."

A piece of metal fell out of the side of his head onto the couch, covered in blood. The both of them stared at the piece of metal covered in blood. It rose up into the air and took off, breaking through the window and flying off into the sky.

CHAPTER 4:

DESTRUCTION

The day had come and April was moving into her new home. Darkside and his friends were all there to help. As they were unloading the boxes, Trinity's brother made the comment saying, "Jeez Jasmine! You sure have a lot of stuff! How could one person have so much junk?"

She replied to him, "It's not junk! It's my clothes!"

He laughed. "Does one person really need that much clothing? Come on, you could probably open your own store with all this."

April crossed her arms. "It's a girl thing." She said.

Meanwhile back in Phoenix, Arizona, the clone of Darkside was walking the streets. He walked into a police station and walked up to the front desk. The woman at the desk asked, "How may I help you?"

"You can surrender. All of you can." The clone said.

"What do you mean?" She asked in surprise.

"All of you can give up now. Surrender or there will be bloodshed." The clone ordered.

An officer stood up and said, "Who do you think you are?"

He replied to the officer with a smug look on his face, "I am the one who will be killing all of you fools today." As everybody was in a bit of a panic and the room fell eerily quiet, the clone reached over and grabbed the lady behind the desk by the neck. He snapped her neck instantly. Two police officers drew their weapons and pointed them at the clone. One of the officers ordered him to get down, but the clone laughed and approached one of the officers.

"Don't move!" One of the officers yelled. The clone continued to approach the officer. The nervous officer yelled out, "I told you, don't fucking move!" The officer fired a shot. It did nothing and merely bounced harmlessly off the clone's head.

Everyone stood in shock and two more officers drew their guns and now all four officers opened fire on the clone. The clone dropped down to one knee and then stood right back up and said, "Did you guys think that was gonna stop me?" The clone leapt toward one of the officers tackling him to the ground. As he was mounted on top of the officer the clone took his hand, stuck it straight through the officer's chest and pulled his heart directly out. The clone dropped the officer's still heart on the floor and licked the blood off his hand.

The clone turned around and commanded everyone else "Run." Nobody hesitated, and every single human in the room bailed out at full speed. As the clone was standing in the abandoned station by himself, a phone rang nearby. He picked up the receiver to the phone. "Hello?"

There was a lady on the phone who frantically said, "911! I just witnessed a murder!"

The clone laughed and replied, "I just committed murder." And slammed the phone receiver down. Outside of the police station, there was a man walking by talking on his cell phone. He stopped in front of the police station and was arguing with a person on the other line. Suddenly the entire building blew up. The man was knocked back into the street and from the rubble and the fire emerged the clone, unscathed.

Back at Jasmine's house, as they were all continuing to help her unpack into her new home, Trinity's brother's phone went off. He answered the phone and a shocked look appeared on his face. "Okay I'll be there..." He said, and then hung up.

Chaos asked, "Who was that?"

He replied, "I just got a call from my boss. He said there was a monster attacking downtown Phoenix. I'm gonna have to take off and check it out."

Trinity asked, "Do you want me to come with you?"

He replied, "Naw, I've got this. I'll be sure to call you guys if I need some help."

Darkside cut in, saying, "Hopefully you don't need our help, I was planning on taking a nap later!"

Trinity's brother bolted out the front door and took off running.

Back in Phoenix, the clone walked to a shopping mall. He stood outside the front doors. People were in panic and he yelled out, "Everybody get down!!!" Everybody dropped down to the ground in fear. The clone yelled, "I want somebody to get the president here. You all have thirty minutes to make it happen before heads start rolling. After thirty minutes, for every minute on the minute that he isn't here, I will kill one person." The clone looked over at the clock sign on the side of the mall and announced, "Your time starts now."

People frantically dialed emergency numbers in their cell phones while the clone stood there. A couple of minutes had passed. After ten minutes, he yelled out, "Never mind, I've changed my mind. I'm going to start killing people until the president shows up." There was a family laying on the ground. The clone walked up to them, grabbed a little girl by the neck and stood her up.

The father yelled out, "NO! That's my daughter! Please, leave her alone!!!"

The clone looked into the little girl's eyes while he held her by the throat. He asked her, "Where is the president, little girl?"

As she was frightened and crying, she hysterically replied, "I don't know!!!"

The father cried out again, "Please don't hurt my daughter!"

The clone looked down at him and asked, "How much do you love your daughter?"

The man replied, "I love her very much! Please don't hurt her!"

The clone smiled and said, "That's a nice answer but it's not the one I'm looking for." And then he flung her back into the farthest wall of the building. She hit the wall, her head busting, and she hit the ground. The man began to cry over the fact that his beloved daughter was dead.

The clone then grabbed him by the throat and lifted him up effortlessly. He looked down at the man's little boy and asked, "How much do you love your father?"

"Please don't hurt my daddy!" The little boy shrieked.

There was a security guard that stood up from the ground and yelled, "Leave those people alone!"

The clone turned and glared at the guard, then said, "What do we have here? Not even a real law enforcement officer. Just a rent-a-cop who wants to play a hero. You just made the dumbest mistake of your life. I will spare the family but I will take your life instead!" The clone dropped the man and walked over to the security guard. He was frozen in fear as the clone approached him.

The clone grabbed the guard by the neck, pulled him in close and asked him, "Are you ready to die?"

The guard reached for his belt, grabbed a can of mace and sprayed the clone in his eyes. He became furious by the guard's foolish mistake. He flung the guard into the farthest wall as he had done to the little girl.

A group of police cars pulled into the parking lot. A helicopter hovered above the mall, where everything was taking place. A squad of soldiers dropped out of the helicopter via a rope and entered the mall through the roof. These four soldiers bounded up to the clone. A small group of police officers crept around to get to where the clone was as well. One of the soldiers yelled, "Open fire!!!" All four of them opened fire on the clone.

Instantly the clone too off and was right in front of one of the soldiers and grabbed him by the neck. With one hand, he lifted the soldier into the air as the other soldiers continued to shoot him, their bullets ricocheting harmlessly off of his body. The clone snapped the soldier's neck and dropped him to the ground.

One of the officers from the group of police hurried over to the clone and she shot him in the back of the head. The clone turned around with a furious expression on his face, lifted up his right hand and held his palm out to her and yelled, "DIE!!!" A blaze of fire came from his hand similarly to a flamethrower.

She dropped to the ground, her body set aflame, and the clone grabbed her by her left ankle. He picked her up, swung her overhead and slammed her into the ground, and while still holding her ankle swung her body overhead again and slammed her into the ground on his opposite side.

Still holding onto her ankle he lifted her up a little bit, then threw a straight kick to her upper chest. He lifted her higher by her leg, then let go of her ankle. While she fell he delivered a strong kick to her sternum, forcing her body to fly like a rag doll across the mall.

Suddenly it began to get very windy. The clone looked over to his left, and Michael Smith had arrived to the battlefield. The clone began his arrogant approach to Michael. As this was going on, a black van pulled up to the side of the mall and four men got out of the back of the van. Their faces were covered up with masks. One of them was carrying what looked to be a body bag.

They had rushed over to where the female officer was. The flames had died down along with her but her mangled body had cuts over it and broken bones protruding out of her legs. Two of them picked her up. One of the others put the bag down and placed her body inside and zipped it up.

The four men picked up her body in the bag and quickly retreated to the van. They placed her body in the back and closed the door. There was another man in the driver's seat. He picked up a cell phone and said, "Subject acquired. Project X-75 is under way." The van then drove down the road at a high speed.

CHAPTER 5:

THE BATTLE BEGINS

As the clone walked up to Michael, he had a confused look on his face. In shock, Michael had said, "What the… You look just like my friend!"

The clone stopped right in front of him. Michael, in shock, said, "How is this possible? How do you look like my friend!?"

The clone replied, "I'm not your brother. I'm the more improved fighter."

Still with a shocked look, Michael was absolutely speechless. The clone looked at him. Everybody was silent. The clone began to walk circles around Michael. He didn't take his eyes off the clone as he circled Michael. The clone then said, "Michael Smith… The hero of the people. The savior! The protector of the weak. You don't fool me! You may fool all these people, but I see right through you. I know Michael Smith isn't your real name. I also know that you aren't from this planet. I also know that you cannot beat me. And what you need to know is that today is the day you die."

He replied to the clone, "You're right. My name isn't Michael and I'm not from here. But you're wrong. I WILL stop you!"

The clone just laughed. "You're not gonna stop me. I don't even know why I should waste my time fighting you. Fighting you would only be a warm up. But as you can probably tell, I'm already warmed up. So if you value your life and desire to live, I suggest you call the strong one because I know it is not you."

Michael Smith replied to the clone, "I'll show you how strong I am!" He threw a right hook and hit the clone in the face, but he didn't move. Another right hook; the clone simply continued to stand unaffected. He threw a third right hook but the clone caught his fast in his hand.

Michael was in awe of how strong this clone of Darkside was. Just as the evil clone did to the others before him, he flung him into the building wall at full speed. As Michael was starting to stand up, the clone was standing right in front of him. "This is your last chance!!! Call the strong one!"

As Michael stood up he said, "You haven't beat me yet. I'm not calling anybody!"

He grabbed him by the neck and told Michael "Wrong answer!!!" He lifted Michael. As he dangled in the air, he threw a hard knee into the clone's sternum. He just laughed as he held Michael by the neck." I guess you have decided to die, such a bad choice. All these people are going to lose the hero that they love so much. Is that what you want? Do you want to let all of them down? Well, I guess you already did. After all, you can't stop me!"

The clone let go and he fell to the ground. As Michael was in pain he pulled out his phone and called Chaos. As they had just finished unpacking all of the boxes, Chaos's phone started to ring. He picked up.

"Hello, Chaos, it's me. This monster is to strong. I need help..... He looks just like Darkside, very strong get here fast."

Chaos replied, "What? He looks like my brother? Don't worry we are on the way."

As Chaos put away his phone, he told the others what was going on. Darkside was in shock, "I can't believe that the monster looks like me he said."

"I can't believe it myself," Chaos said. "But that's what he said. We need to get there fast! I don't know how long he will last against this look alike of you brother."

As they all took off to go to Phoenix and help in the fight against the clone, there was a man in an office with a group of other people. There was a meeting going on. The man that was the boss was giving a huge lecture to all of his workers. The man yelled out, "I am tired of ALL of this!!! I'm looking for results and all I'm getting is excuses! We're losing money on this deal.

You guys need to get your shit together and make this happen! I don't give a damn if we have to be here all night. I don't give a damn if we have to work through holidays! I will cancel every person's vacation in here until the end of the year until this is done! I don't care if your son or daughter has school events, I don't care about any church or family functions or events either! You all work here, and you work for me! So people, let's get back to work and we're gonna finish this project and you can forget about going to lunch because you'll be working through it!"

A man at a table rose his hand and said, "But my wife is nine months pregnant! I really need to be with her!"

The boss replied, "Pregnant or not, I don't care if she's dying. You're here to work, or you can pack up your shit and leave!"

Everyone in the office was shocked of how angry and hateful their boss was. They all were afraid of his wrath. As their boss stood there, his face was so red – a face full of ire and anger. Suddenly he dropped to his knees and began holding his head in pain. Everyone was in shock by what was going on. A small piece of metal fell out of the back of his head and onto the ground.

The pain went away, and the man stood back up. The piece of metal dripping in blood lifted up off the ground. The boss was so scared that he collapsed and was in a panic. The piece of metal took off through a glass window and flew into the sky.

Meanwhile back at the Phoenix Mall, the clone of Darkside looked down at Michael and said, "You made the right decision. And all this time I thought you were stupid! I guess you're not as dumb as I thought you were. So since you made the right decision I'm going to let you walk away."

Michael had a shocked look on his face. The clone started to laugh. "I'm just kidding." The clone said. "I'm going to kill you! If you believed me you're really stupid. After all I am the bad guy and now you're going to die."

As Michael was in a panic at his final moments and that his sister and the others would not make it there in time, he stood up as fast as he could but the monster just knocked him back down to the ground. As he tried to crawl away to get distance from the monster, the clone walked right behind him. The clone spoke out to him, "So this is the great hero, crawling away like a scared child!

You know all these people look up to you, and now it's going to go down in history that the great Michael Smith is crawling away like the coward he is instead of dying an honorable death by staying and fighting! What a shame.

As Michael continued to crawl, he jumped up and ran to the side of the building. The clone of his friend laughed and continued to walk slowly to where Michael ran to. As Michael ran around to the side of the building he tried to hide behind a garbage can. He thought to himself, "Man this is a really crappy situation! I hope they get here fast! I definitely can't take this guy.

He's too strong!" While he continued to hide, he heard the clone call out, "Michael, Michael? Where are you…? You know you can't hide from me forever… Why don't you just come out and meet your maker?"

As all of this was going on, there was a press conference taking place in Seattle, Washington. Crystal Jones and Arthur Quebec were giving speeches about their new breakthrough product. Arthur was on stage giving the presentation.

As he spoke about the new breakthrough, "Ladies and gentlemen, thank you for joining us here today. I'm Arthur Quebec and this is my colleague Crystal Jones, and we have exciting news for you today. As you all know, we have been working on a new drug that will help heal wounds, correct damaged ligaments, and any other problems the human body may encounter. We have been running many tests on both animal and human subjects and my colleague and I are happy to report to you that they are a success. Crystal will give you the rest of the information. Thank you very much!"

Crystal stepped up to speak. "Good afternoon everyone." She said. "Just as my colleague Arthur had mentioned we have a breakthrough on the drug that will repair human life. There will be no more injuries, no more broken bones, no more muscles or tears that can't be healed to 100 percent. As you all know, when a bone is broken it can heal and be used just as it was before the damage but it's never truly the same as it was before the damage. This new drug, 'Lifeline', will give you the chance to continue living your life just as if the damage never happened.

"Now you may be wondering… What are the side-effects? Everything has side-effects, right? And you're right. Even this new drug has side-effects. Now I know what you're thinking, 'this is too good to be true'. There are many side-effects and probably outrageous ones.

But I'm happy to tell you all that there is only one side-effect. That is, it may cause you to want to lead a more active lifestyle than you already do. The new drug will be available in pharmacies and hospitals everywhere in a week! Are there any questions?"

A man in the back of the crowd asked, "So you're basically telling us that you can repair any issue with human life, any damages to a hundred percent without there being any real side-effect?"

Crystal replied, "Yes."

As the man sat down, another man stood up and asked, "So you have found a way to play God?"

Crystal replied, "It is not that we are playing God, we are just improving life. We are not playing God, nor creating life, but just improving it."

The man had a look of disbelief on his face, and said, "It sounds like you're trying to play God to me. I'm all for making life better, but it sounds like you're trying to play God."

Crystal replied again, "Sir, we are not trying to play God, nor have we ever wanted to play God. Our intent here is simply to improve life."

Arthur Quebec then stepped in and said, "We just want to make one thing clear: That we are not trying to play God, as Crystal had mentioned. This drug will be available to anybody who decides to use it, and for the right reasons. Nobody has an obligation to use this drug if they are injured or sick in any way.

Just as if you go to the store, you are not obligated to buy anything you don't want or that you feel are unnecessary. So does anybody have any questions that are more relevant to Lifeline?"

As the press conference continued on, Michael was hiding behind a dumpster and the clone walked over in front of him. "There you are!" He exclaimed. "Are you done hiding? Are you ready to continue? Or do I need to look the other way so you can run and hide with more shame? I bet you're hoping that you can drag this out long enough until the others get here. As I think about it, it would be nice to just hurry up and kill you but it would also be nice to kill you in front of your family. What do you think, Michael?"

Michael replied back to the clone, "If you were truly gonna kill me you would have already did it. I bet you can't kill me. You don't have enough power. That's why you haven't done it yet."

The clone laughed. "I could have killed you very easily! I should just kill you right now for running your mouth."

Michael leapt forward and head-butted the clone, knocking him off balance. He then wrapped his arms around the clone and dove into the air and the clone began to laugh as they continued rising into the air the clone uttered "What's next? Let me guess, you're gonna drop me from the sky? Maybe throw a couple of punches and a head-butt?"

Michael released his hold from the clone, took a step back and threw a right hook at him. The punch had no effect as the clone simply laughed. The clone then grabbed Michael by the throat with his right hand and pushed him into the ground as he held onto him.

The two hit the ground and as the ground cracked from the impact and the clone released his grip on his neck and stood up. Out of nowhere, Trinity came flying with a kick. The clone grabbed her by the ankle just before she could make contact and slammed her into the ground. He looked down at her and said, "You're not the strong one! Where is the strong one??? I don't have time to be messing around with the rest of you."

Trinity stood up. Michael began to stand as well but was badly injured and having trouble getting to his feet. A voice cried out, "Hey!!!" The clone looked to his right and he saw Darkside and Chaos walking towards him.

CHAPTER 6:

THE BROKEN HEARTED

As the battle with the clone was about to heat up, Crystal and Arthur were at a restaurant having dinner. Arthur said to her, "Today was a success. This new breakthrough will change the way people live their lives and also make us very rich."

She smiled back at him and said, "Work, work... I don't want to talk about work right now. I wanna talk more about us."

He replied, "Yes, I know."

She continued smiling at him. He seemed to grow a little uncomfortable. She then said, "I can't wait for our wedding day."

He smiled and said, "Me too…" and then looked away.

Back in Phoenix, Darkside and his brother walked up to the clone. With great shock Darkside said, "Wow…! This guy looks just like me! I can't believe it…"

The clone just laughed. As Darkside seemed to be more amazed than ready for battle, the clone spoke out. "It's about time! I've been tired of wasting my time with all of these imbeciles."

Darkside replied to him, "I know we're here to stop you, but man!!! I'd have to say this is a really good copy! It's so identical!"

Chaos then said, "Brother, I know you're enjoying the moment but we need to stop this guy…"

Darkside replied to Chaos, "I know, I know. It's just amazing how detailed it is! He literally looks like somebody made a photocopy!"

The clone yelled out, "SHUT UP!!! I didn't come here to do a comparison. I came here to fight you and take over the world. And YOU are the only one standing in my way. These people you brought with you are just pawns! Now prepare to DIE!!!"

He replied to the clone, "You're right. We need to hurry up and get this over with. I don't want it to cut into my nap time." Trinity and her brother looked at each other and shook their head in disbelief. Darkside then said,

"Okay you guys, give us some space. You guys can sit this one out. I'll take care of this copycat."

Trinity's brother asked, "Are you sure??? I just fought with this guy and he's very strong."

He replied, "I'm sure. This won't take too long. He may look like me, but he doesn't fight like me."

The clone smiled and the others began to step back to give them some space. The clone stepped right up to Darkside. As the two were face-to-face staring in each other's eyes not moving a muscle and while Chaos and the others were looking on and everyone else in the mall was staring in anticipation, Darkside and the clone both took two steps back. The clone then threw a right hook.

Darkside blocked it. He retaliated to this attack by throwing a hard right hook, but the clone blocked it. They both stopped for the moment and stared at each other, then both smiled.

Suddenly the clone leapt forward and head-butted Darkside, knocking him off balance. He grabbed Darkside by the neck and jumped into the air with him. While the two were flying into the air Darkside hooked his legs around the clone's body, and used his arm to break the hold the clone had around his neck. Darkside leaned back with his legs wrapped around the clone and flung him towards the ground hard. As the clone fell Darkside dove after him.

The clone landed on his feet and Darkside tackled him into the ground. He then wrapped both of his hands around the clone's neck and picked him up. The clone had a smile on his face. As Darkside let go of his neck, he simultaneously kneed him in the gut. The clone bent over but still had the smile on his face. Darkside dropped his elbow to the back of the clone's neck. He then grabbed the clone by the arm and tossed him into the building. The clone hit the building with hellacious force and broke straight through the wall. He then quickly ran to where the clone had landed, and the clone leapt out of the rubble and attacked Darkside. They traded punches and kicks left and right.

Trinity looked over at Chaos. "Wow, it seems they fight pretty even, don't you think?" She asked.

He replied, "I'm not too sure. It seems like it's pretty even and I'm sure both of them are holding back. This is gonna be a hard one to call. I don't know how he was cloned from my brother but it seems he does possess the same skills as him." As they continued to look on, the clone threw a kick to Darkside's side and it seemed to knock him a bit off balance. The clone then grabbed Darkside by the head with both hands and pulled his face down into the clone's knee.

He held onto Darkside's head and did this two more times. He then head-butted Darkside. Darkside began to stumble and almost fell over. The clone then did a boot-to-face, knocking Darkside down. The clone stomped on his sternum, grinding his heel into him.

"This is pretty sad... I was expecting more out of you." The clone taunted.

He replied, "I guess you must have forgot: I'm the original, and you're the copy." With that, he knocked the clone's foot off of him, leapt up and put him into a sleeper hold. As he started to choke the clone, he jumped into the air. He paused for the moment as he held his grip firmly around the clone's neck. Darkside dove straight into the ground as he held onto the clone and they both hit the ground. Darkside stood on top of the clone's back. As the clone laid face-down, he stomped his left foot onto the back of the clone's head, shoving his face further into the concrete floor.

Darkside took a knee right next to the clone and grabbed him by the back of the neck and lifted him out of the ground. The clone had yet another smile on his face and slammed the clone's face back into the ground. Darkside lifted him up again, so Darkside repeated the motion with increased force. He then let go of the hold, stood up and grabbed the clone by his left ankle.

Darkside began to walk slowly, dragging the clone's limp body behind him. He finally stopped, walked back over to the clone, and lifted him up. He still had a smile on his face, so Darkside slammed the clone's face back into the ground again. He lifted the clone up one more time to see if he was still smiling and surprisingly there was no smile on the clone's face this time.

The clone then said, "Fuck you." He elbowed Darkside right in the throat, making him release the grip he had on the clone's neck. Before he could react, the clone stood up and kneed Darkside right in the face.

Darkside fell over and the clone began to stomp repeatedly on his body. The clone yelled out, "I'm just getting started!" The clone then lifted up his foot and was going to stomp Darkside right in the face. As it came down, Darkside caught the foot with one hand.

Meanwhile Crystal was on her way back to the hotel. She had a bag in her hand. She walked through the hotel door and up to her room. As she made her way to the room she had no idea what she was about to witness.

Crystal walked in and heard the shower running and quickly started to get undressed and she changed into some seductive lingerie. As she was standing there at the foot of the bed, the bathroom door opened and Arthur came walking out. He had a shocked look on his face. She called out to him, "Hey there, Arthur, I've heard you've been a bad, bad, boy… but I've been very naughty myself and I need to be punished…" She turned and bent over the bed.

In shock he replied, "I didn't know you were coming back so soon!"

She replied sensually, "I decided I didn't want to wait and decided it was time for my punishment…" She then turned and looked behind her and suddenly a woman in a towel walked out of the bathroom and stood behind Arthur. She couldn't believe her eyes, and stood up, turned around, and yelled angrily, "What the fuck?!"

He said to her, "I can explain…" She just stared at him. Before he could speak, the woman behind him said something.

"Is this the woman that you were talking about? She doesn't really look like she's all that."

Very angrily, Crystal yelled, "Shut up! How could you do this to me??? We're getting married!"

He replied, "It is true… I wanted to marry you. But I don't love you. The only reason I've been with you these past two years is because I needed your help on the Lifeline project.

The girl behind him just laughed and interjected, "Somebody just got dumped!" in a mock-song.

Emotions welled up in Crystal and she began to cry hard. She threw on her coat, grabbed her things and stormed out. The other woman then put her arms around Arthur. They both smiled and then walked into the bedroom.

Back in Phoenix, the fight continued between Darkside and his clone. Darkside had him pinned into the wall. He said out to the clone, "Have you had enough?"

The clone began to laugh. He then reached out and put his hand on Darkside's shoulder. He whispered to him, "I'm feeling just fine. How about you?"

Darkside then grabbed the clone by the arm, pulled him out of the wall and into the ground. The clone stood up very slowly and looked at Darkside. "I'm beginning to get bored. I think it's time to shake it up a little bit." He then grabbed Darkside by the shoulders and flew up into the air with him.

He had made his way around the back of Darkside and said, "That location was boring! How about we take this more downtown?" As they flew deeper into the city, the clone released him. Darkside fell but landed on his feet. The two of them were standing in the middle of traffic and cars stopped and began honking angrily at them.

A woman rolled her window down and yelled with her head out, "What are you two assholes doing? Get the hell out of the road!"

The clone looked at her and replied, "How about YOU get out of the road?"

As she looked at him very angrily, he held up his hand, pointing it at the woman in the car. He dropped his hand down to his side and simultaneously the woman's car was pulled towards the floor, flattening it while she was inside. The clone then said, "Is there anyone else who would like to interrupt?" The people all began to panic, left their vehicles and ran off in fear.

Darkside ran to the clone and the clone ran to him. They both met head-on and aggressively exchanged punches once again. Chaos and the others had followed and were watching from a distance. While the two continued trading blows, the clone threw a right hook but Darkside blocked it, grabbed him by the arm and tossed him into a truck. As the clone's body was indented into the side of the truck, Darkside tackled him straight through it.

While they laid on the ground on the other side of the truck, the clone turned the tables and was now on top of Darkside. He grabbed him and stood him up on his feet, and pushed him into the wall of a building nearby. Darkside lifted his leg, kicking the clone off of him and forcing him to release his grip.

He ran right for the clone but the clone side-stepped him and kicked him in the back. He then turned around and the clone tackled him and mounted him, then started punching him in the face with hook punches, then asked tauntingly, "Aren't you having fun?"

As he continued to hit Darkside in the face Darkside stopped moving. Chaos yelled out, "BROTHER!!!" And dove straight for them. The clone then stopped punching Darkside and right as Chaos was about to hit him, he threw an elbow that hit Chaos right in the face.

The clone stood up, turned and looked at Chaos and said, "I didn't wanna fight you, but if you wanna butt in to my business I guess I can kill you too."

As Darkside laid on the ground, he said, "Your fight is with ME!" When the clone turned to look at him, Darkside spring boarded off the ground and tackled the clone. As they hit the ground, Darkside looked up at his brother and said, "It's okay! I got this."

Chaos replied to him, "We should all fight him together!"

But Darkside said, "No."

Chaos then walked back over to the others. The clone said to him, "Now that's more like it!" Darkside stood up away from the clone. The clone slowly got up and said, "Well that was very nice of you, and also letting me get up. I might have to return the favor next time I knock you into the ground."

Darkside grabbed the clone by the throat and pulled him close. "There isn't gonna be a next time." He rasped. The clone smiled once again. Darkside threw the clone into another abandoned vehicle in the road.

Darkside ran to the clone and as he was running, the clone yelled out, "Darkside Blast!!!" A powerful blast came from the clone's hand and it hit Darkside dead-on. Chaos and the others were in shock as Darkside disappeared in the blast.

The clone started laughing. As the blast ended and the clone put his hand down, he started walking over to Chaos and the others. As he approached, he said, "That's gotta suck! Done in by your own move!"

As he continued to walk over to them, Darkside came out from nowhere and punched the clone right in the back. The clone then stopped, turned around, and stared into Darkside's eyes. He began to laugh once more.

CHAPTER 7:

A WOMAN SCORNED

As the clone stood in front of Darkside and continued to laugh, he said out to him, "This is just great!!! We are equally matched! Old school versus new school! You do know everything has its time. I've been holding back this whole time, and now I'm going to kill you all." The clone continued to laugh.

Darkside then turned his back to him and started to walk away. The clone stopped laughing and growled, "You dare to turn your back to me and walk away!? You're just like Michael Smith! A coward!"

As Darkside continued to walk away from the clone, the clone took off and ran towards him. Just as the clone was about to attack him, Darkside threw an elbow, catching the clone right between the eyes. The clone began to reel and turned around. Darkside head-butted the clone, making him stumble. Darkside launched a right hook and nailed the clone right between the eyes. He then kicked the clone right in the stomach. The clone dropped to one knee and Darkside walked over, grabbed him by the back of the neck and stood him up. The clone then reached out, grabbed Darkside by the neck and flung him into another nearby building. With Darkside partially indented into the brick building, the clone began to start steaming. His eyes began to turn bright red.

The clone spoke very angrily. "Now die, you little worm!!!" He yelled. As he roared, a blast of energy came straight out of his mouth and hit Darkside head-on. While the blast began to destroy the building, Chaos and the others began to panic.

Chaos said, "I haven't seen that move since my father used it!" The building continued to crumble and fall apart while Darkside flew straight through the blast and grabbed the clone by the throat with his left hand and began to choke him. As he held the clone by the neck, he used his right hand and stuck it straight through the clone's chest, ripping out his spine through the entry wound. Blood began to spew out of the clone's mouth. Darkside dropped the spine.

Then with his hand covered in blood he held his palm in front of the clone's face and said, "You spineless monster… Remember, you're just an imitation. I'm the real deal. Let me show you how it's done! Darkside BLAAAST!!!" The familiar beam of energy came out of Darkside's palm and hit the clone in the face. The clone stopped moving. The blast had ceased. Darkside put his hands down. The headless body of the clone fell over. Darkside then kicked the spine of the clone over to the body, pointed the palm of his right hand at the body, and blasted them both, disintegrating the remains of them both.

As Darkside walked over to his brother and friends, Chaos said, "That was unbelievable… I have to be honest, brother, there were a few times I thought you were gonna lose…"

Darkside laughed and replied, "I told you! I had everything under control. And besides, he was a copy of me. And who knows ME better than ME?"

Chaos laughed and they all walked away together.

As the police and people of the city were coming back to rebuild the damage from the fight, a reporter came up to the group and asked Michael Smith what happened. He replied to the reporter, "As you guys saw, Stan Jones had created a Fear monster that we took down a couple of months ago.

This time he came back with a new creation. I don't know how but he created a duplicate of my good friend. The man you see here isn't the bad guy, he's a hero. And you all need to know that it was not me that defeated the evil copy."

The reporter asked, "So all of four of you guys are superheroes?"

Trinity cut in and said, "Well we all are pretty awesome."

Michael then said, "The truth is all of us are incredibly strong, and we are not from this planet. We left home to come here and start a new life and never guessed that the terror that went on the past couple of months would happen. We never planned to be heroes, we just wanted to fit in and live our lives. But what's done is done. You can all rest assured that anything happens, we will be here to stop it."

The reporter asked, "So you decided to sit this one out and let your friend handle it?"

He replied, "I could not beat the evil copy. Also, my name isn't Michael Smith. That was just a name that I was using to try and fit in. But as long as everybody knows the truth I want you all to know my real name. This is my sister Trinity, as you all know. This is Chaos, that's his brother Darkside, and I am Messiah."

The reporter looked at the camera and said, "Ladies and Gentlemen, there you have it. Michael Smith, or Messiah, as he is actually known, and his friends and family."

There was a man who walked into a bank. He walked up to the counter. The teller said to him, "Hello sir, how may I help you?"

The man said, "Good evening! How are you doing?"

The woman replied, "Just fine. What can I do for you today?"

The man pulled a nine millimeter pistol out and pointed it at the lady. "I'm here to make a withdrawal." He said and smiled. The woman screamed. "There's no reason to scream. I just want the money. Nobody move or this pretty little redhead is getting a bullet in between the eyes. So everybody, get the fuck down and all of the tellers empty out their registers! Hey you, fat ass! Yeah, you! The security guard! Make your lard-ass useful and get my money ready!"

Two other guys came into the bank, each one with an AK 47 rifle slung around their shoulder. One ran around to the back and another went to the side to follow the security guard, who was on his way to the vault. The man that was holding the nine millimeter continued to have it held on the woman. "Looks like that bag's getting full but we're gonna need more money. Find another sack for me, honey!" He winked at her as he finished the sentence.

The woman very nervously bent over to pick up another bag. The man smiled and said, "Not bad from behind, lady! Not bad…" As she stood up and started to fill the bag, there was a security button on the floor. She stepped on it as she continued to fill the new bag. The man looked at her as he continued to point the gun. He said, "You're very pretty!" He looked at her name tag and said, "You are very pretty, Yvonne. I wanted to let you live, but I know what you just did." She had a look of panic on her face. He pulled the trigger and shot her between the eyes.

The woman fell back lifeless, and her body struck the ground hard. The man looked around and said, "I know the cops are on the way, so we're gonna make this quick. So nobody else do anything stupid, like Yvonne, unless you want lead in your face."

He waved the gun around. "Anybody else? Anybody? No? Didn't think so. It's too bad that Yvonne could not be as smart as the rest of you guys and decided not to live."

Soon enough they collected all the money. As they made their exit out of the bank, the man had said, "Thank you for your cooperation. It's too bad that everybody did not get to live today but I will do something…" He took a twenty dollar bill out of his pocket and dropped it on the floor and then said, "Somebody make sure that Yvonne's family gets some flowers. My condolences." The three men quickly left the building and leapt into a black van with no windows and it tore down the street.

One of the guys said to the leader, "Hell yeah! That was the best heist we pulled. We got a lot of money this time. I can't wait to get my cut, we each get a pretty generous share!"

The man that was the leader laughed. "Split three ways, huh? I'm the brains of the operation here. I'm taking half and you two can have twenty-five percent each."

The man replied back to him, "That's not fair! We had a deal. We were splitting this all equally!"

He said, "Boys don't get too mad, the boss always gets the bigger cut!" And he began to laugh.

The driver of the truck said, "Damn. Why you gotta be like that?"

The boss said, "Because that's just how it is boys. Maybe someday when you're a boss you'll get the bigger cut."

Suddenly the man began yelling out in pain, grabbing his head. The two partners both asked him in worry what was wrong. "I don't know!" He responded. "I feel like my head's about to explode!!!" Suddenly a metal piece fell out of the side of his face, onto his lap. As the pain went away, everybody was shocked and were quiet as they drove down the road. The piece of metal covered in his blood lifted off the ground and shot out of the window.

They all looked at each other and stayed quiet as they drove off.

Meanwhile, Crystal was back home in Los Angeles. It was night time and she was crying her eyes out as she was curled up on the couch eating ice cream out of a container. She was watching a movie. As she continued to cry, she looked over at the picture she had on the mantle of her and Arthur together and kept on crying.

The movie that she was watching was of a man and a woman fighting at home. As she continued to watch this film, the husband and wife on TV that were fighting and the woman on the screen said to her husband, "I'm not gonna take this abuse anymore!" She slapped him.

The man was angry, grabbed her by the throat and pushed her into the counter of the kitchen. As the man was choking her, the woman in the movie grabbed a knife and stabbed her stomach and broke the hold he had on her neck. The movie went to a commercial break and she saw a commercial for the upcoming drug, Lifeline.

While Crystal sat there watching the commercial, she grew angry and said aloud, "I'm not taking this either…" She got up, grabbed her jacket and walked out the door.

She had went to the lab and used her ID badge to get in. The security guard said, "Hey, Miss Jones! What are you doing here? It's so late."

She replied with a smile, "Oh I just forgot something in the office. I came to pick it up real quick."

The guard replied, "Okay, you have a nice night Ms. Jones." He nodded at her and walked off.

She continued making her way into the lab and opened the case where the sample of pills were there. She took a key from inside and grabbed a few bottles, stuffing her purse with them. She walked to another room with the key and opened up a cabinet and went up to a bunch of tubes with a blue liquid inside. She took all four of them and walked off into a back room. Soon enough, it was morning and the sun was coming up.

The security guard was making his rounds and walked through. He was preparing to turn the lights in the lab off, when he heard a noise. He stopped and walked into the lab and saw the cabinets open. He saw an open back door and walked inside cautiously. He said, "Miss Jones, is that you?"

She turned and looked at him with a sinister smile on her face. She had a giant needle in her hand and a tourniquet around her left arm just below the elbow. She opened and closed her hand to make the veins visible.

"What's going on? What are you doing ma'am?" The guard asked.

She replied, "Something I should have done a long time ago." She then injected herself with the needle.

"What are you doing!?" The guard cried out. She dropped the needle and fell to the ground and began convulsing. The guard rushed over to her side. "Miss Jones! Miss Jones what's wrong? Are you all right?" Her body suddenly stopped moving. He set her down and checked for a pulse at her throat. He shook his head as he thought she was dead. He pulled out his cell phone and dialed 911 and spoke over the phone, "I just witnessed a suicide."

Suddenly Crystal started to move again. He was in shock and she grabbed him by the neck. She stood up and lifted him as he gasped for air. As the two were standing and she was choking him, she said very angrily, "No man will ever hurt me EVER again!" Soon enough, the man stopped moving, and his body became lifeless. She released her hold from his neck, and his body dropped to the ground. She stood there for a moment looking down at the dead body of the man. She then smiled and walked off.

Full of hate, Crystal made her way back home. She started packing up her clothes and a few other items. As this was going on, Darkside and the others were back at April's place. They were having a cookout. They were celebrating April's 25th birthday. April had said, "Man I just started going back to school and it's been killer. I know I'm going to school online but it's just so much homework and too many chapters to read."

Her sister commented, "Well it's good that you're going back to school! It's been a while since you've been out on your extended break, huh?"

April smiled and replied, "Yeah, took three years off. I need to go back and get this done. I kinda wish now that I could have gone to school for something different besides law."

Her sister replied back, "Well one day you'll make a great lawyer and you won't be working in a bank as a teller anymore."

April laughed. "I know. It's just so much reading. I don't want to read all of these books, it's just way too much."

Darkside then cut in. "Well why don't we just read them all at once?"

With a confused look on her face April asked, "What do you mean?"

"Where are all the books you are supposed to read?" Darkside asked. "We can get this done really fast."

She went inside and came back out with four hardcover books all stacked on top of each other. She said, "These are all of the books I have to read for the semester. It's boring and I definitely don't want to read all this. It's just an overload for me and I can't do it."

As the books were stacked on each other on the table, Darkside walked up to the book stack and placed his hand on them. The books began to glow a bright green. April and her sister were shocked by this action. Soon enough the books stopped glowing and Darkside had a funny look on his face.

Darkside said, "Wow, that WAS boring." He then walked over to April and put the same hand he touched the books with on her forehead. His hand started to glow as it did when he placed it on the books. His hand stopped glowing before long and he took his hand off of her head. "What are you thinking?" He asked her.

With a look of shock on her face she said, "I can't believe it! I know everything in the books!" Darkside started to laugh.

He said, "One ability that we all have is that we can touch an object and learn everything about it in a matter of seconds."

She replied, "Thanks."

Trinity was in the background looking at both of them. She had a look of jealousy on her face. Messiah then walked outside with a pan full of ribs. He said, "I love this place! This cookout thing is amazing! We need to start doing this on our home planet! Seems like Earth has all the good stuff!"

As they continued with their cookout, back in central California an earthquake broke out. It was in a small town just outside of San Diego. People were running in fear as the ground cracked and continued to shake. Simultaneously as this was going on, right outside the coast of Florida the weather was starting to get bad. There was a sudden downpour and the streets along that coast were starting to flood.

Emergency sirens warned people to stay indoors. While these natural disasters were simultaneously occurring in California and Florida, Darkside and the others continued with their barbecue, oblivious to these. They had music playing over the radio, and suddenly the song was stopped by a news bulletin.

The radio announcer spoke about the earthquake in California and the hurricane in Florida. Jasmine had made a comment saying, "That's horrible! And kind of weird. How can two natural disasters happen at the exact same time on two different sides of the country?"

Trinity looked over at Messiah and asked, "Still think this place is that great?"

He replied back, "Yeah!!! So what if it rains a little much or the ground shakes in some areas? They got ribs!!!"

She said back, "…Ribs? Really?" A heavy veil of sarcasm was in her tone.

"I'm gonna have to agree with your sister on this one." April said. "You've been here on Earth for almost a year and the thing you love the most is the ribs???"

Messiah then said, "Yeah. Back home, I was just a security guard. Over here, I'm a superhero… AND, I have ribs!

CHAPTER 8:

DISASTERS UNFOLD

It had been two weeks since the defeat of the evil clone of Darkside. Natural disasters were popping up everywhere. New York was currently getting a blizzard. It had been snowing three days nonstop. Power was out in a majority of the state and most people were stranded in their homes, barricaded in their own shelters. The Northwest side of the United States was in a drought.

People in the state of Washington, Oregon, Idaho and Wyoming were getting scorched by a heat wave. The temperature was a hundred and three degrees.

As all this was going on, April was out having lunch with her sister at a local pizza shop. April asked Jasmine, "Why do you look so tired?"

She replied, "I didn't get any sleep last night. I kept hearing weird sounds in my house last night like someone was walking around my hallway and living room. And this morning I could have sworn I heard a woman screaming in the kitchen."

April replied, "Were you watching horror movies again?"

"No, you know I don't like horror movies!!!" Jasmine shot back as though it were obvious.

April laughed and said, "I know you don't like horror movies, Jas. I remember when we were kids and we watched the horror movie about the kids getting killed while they were camping, you didn't sleep for weeks!"

With a bit of an irritated look on her face, Jasmine said, "Stop making fun of me, I don't like that stuff. I don't even have a single horror movie. But... I believe my house is haunted."

April said, "I highly doubt it. I think it's all just in your head."

She replied, "I know I'm not crazy. Just this morning when I left to go meet up with you I had this weird feeling like someone was watching me. Do you think your friends can come over and check it out?"

April said, "Well I can ask them. Trinity and Messiah are busy with their roles as superheroes, I can see if Chaos will do it because I know that Darkside's probably sleeping."

"Ok! Thanks, sis." Jasmine said.

As the two finished their food they then got up to leave. Walking down the street, they ran into a man who was yelling out, "REPENT!!! REPENT!!! SAVE YOURSELVES!!! ACCEPT GOD AS YOUR SAVIOR!!! REPENT!!!"

Jasmine looked at the man and stopped him, then asked him, "What are you talking about?"

The man replied, "My sisters! The end is coming! Haven't you been paying attention to the disasters worldwide? It's not natural! A time of darkness is coming!!! Repent!!! Repent, I tell you! Save yourselves!" The man then ran off immediately, continuing to scream.

The girls looked at each other and April said, "How strange."

"I know, that was so weird." Jasmine said. "He was talking about the end of the world."

She replied, "I wouldn't really believe it but then again in this last year I've seen a lot of things I wouldn't really believe."

As April and her sister got back to April's place, they went inside and as usual Darkside was asleep on the couch. April approached him and called out his name. He didn't respond and so she called out again, "Darkside… Darkside, wake up!"

He still didn't respond, but instead started snoring. Jasmine said, "Maybe we should just ask him later."

April said, "No, we'll ask him now." April then kicked the couch hard. "Darkside!!!"

Darkside jolted awake and said, "What!? I was just sleeping!"

April said, "I need you to go to Jasmine's place because she's hearing a lot of noises. She thinks the place is haunted."

With a confused look on his face, Darkside asked, "Haunted? What do you mean the place is haunted?"

Jasmine spoke saying, "I was hearing weird noises all last night, and this morning it felt like someone was watching me but I was the only person there."

He replied to her, "Okay, well let's go check it out."

The three of them got up and left. As they arrived at Jasmine's place and entered, Jasmine seemed to be very scared. Darkside walked in slowly and walked into the center of the living room and started to look around. Jasmine said, "I heard people walking here and in the hallway and I heard a scream in the kitchen."

April said to her sister, "There's nothing here! I think you were just dreaming. I think maybe you had a nightmare."

"No." Darkside said. "It wasn't a bad dream. There IS something in this house. We're not alone. I can feel the presence of nine others."

With a scared look on her face, "NINE OTHERS???"

Darkside said, "There are twelve people in this house, and three of them are us. Nine others, and I know that they are not friendly. You two get behind me!" As all three of them just stood in the middle of the living room, the front door just shut itself. April and her sister was in total shock.

Darkside continue to look around the room. There was a lamp in one of the corner of the living room. The lamp just fell over, and the girls screamed. Darkside then told them softly to keep clam. As the three of them continue to stand there, all the lights in the whole house started turning themselves on and off. As the light continued to turn on and off, the pictures that was hanging on the wall all fell off one by one.

Darkside called out, "If you are gonna do some, then you should do! Show yourselves!" April asked Darkside if he was crazy, and he said no. "Come on!" He yelled out. The light stopped and stayed on. As the house became very still. April and her sister was holding each other tight.

Suddenly, all the light started turning on and off again. All the doors in the house started to open and shut. As the girls held each other scared to death, Darkside said to them "It's ok, it's ok." There was a set of chairs that was at the kitchen table. One of the chairs lifted up into the air. Then took off right for all three of them. The girls screamed, but before the chair could hit them, Darkside lifted his right arm and knocked it away.

As the doors continued to open and close and the lights continued to flicker, in the kitchen the cabinet drawers opened up. All the silverware came out and was floating in the air. April and her sister were frozen in fear and did not utter a word. The sink turned on and the water began to run out. The shower turned on as well and the water ran.

Suddenly every single window in the house shattered. The floating silverware then flew towards the three of them, but Darkside deflected all of the silverware with his hands.

Darkside said to the girls, "I think you two need to leave. I'll take it from here."

April replied to him, "I don't think they're gonna let us leave!" Suddenly all of the doors stopped moving, the lights all turned off. The house grew silent once again.

April and her sister started walking very slowly to the door. Jasmine tried to open it, but it would not budge. She yelled out frantically, "We're locked in!!!" They both ran right behind Darkside. They then heard footsteps down the hallway. April and her sister held each other for dear life. They started to hear voices in the kitchen and in the bedroom. A man walked out from the hallway.

He looked badly injured and his face was covered in blood as though he were wearing a crimson mask. The man had no eyes; they looked as though they had been cut out. It looked like the flesh was peeled off of his arms. April screamed in horror and then they saw a little boy and a little girl standing in the entrance way to the kitchen.

Darkside yelled out, "That's it? Where's the others six?"

The bloody man with no eyes began to walk slowly towards them. Blood started oozing out from his eye sockets were. Darkside lifted up his right hand and told the man to stop. He continued to move slowly towards him. The man finally stopped right in front of them and Darkside stared at the man. The man uttered the words, "He's coming…"

Darkside replied, "Who's coming?"

The man replied again, "He's coming…" and began to laugh. The lights began to turn on and off once again. As the creature stood there laughing away, Darkside placed his hand on the shoulder of the man. The man began to yell out in pain and faded away. Everything came to a stop in the house.

"Leave now." Darkside told the women. They ran out the front door to the car. Darkside started to glow a bright neon green. He let out a yell and after a little while he stopped glowing. He walked out of the house. The girls were in the car, terrified. He got in the back of the car. When they asked what happened, he replied, "The nine creatures that were in that house were trapped souls. I set them free. Somehow they were bound to your house."

Jasmine, crying out, said, "Bound to the house???"

Darkside said, "Yes. I don't know how, but they were bound to the house. I don't know how but something was holding them there."

April asked, "What did he mean 'He's coming'?"

Darkside said, "I have no idea."

Jasmine said to April, "Well that's it. I'm moving. I'm staying over at your place!"

Soon enough it was nightfall. There was a funeral home on the other side of town. There was a man there working late, getting ready to embalm a body. There lying on the metal slab was a woman. He uncovered the sheet from the woman's body as she lie there, cold and lifeless. He cracked out a joke, saying, "Very nice."

He walked over to a clipboard and picked it up then read off her name. "Susan Miller. Age 29, died of drug overdose. Body was found in an abandoned Dodge

Durango." The man looked back over at the corpse and said, "We have a druggie… and a bimbo. Typical."

He walked back over to the woman's body, grabbed his bone saw and was about to start cutting. Suddenly the woman's hand moved and grabbed his leg. He grabbed her arm and put it back to her side. He said, "No no, miss Miller! Your days of whoring around are over!" He started cutting. As soon as he had cut the Y incision in her torso he began pulling organs out. As he was weighing the organs and inspecting them, he heard a noise and stopped for a moment.

He walked over to the door and opened it, looked around, but saw nobody. He thought to himself, "I'm hearing things…" He closed the door and turned back around. As he started to walk towards the woman, she sat up. Frozen in fear, he stopped. The woman got off of the slab and walked over to him. She stopped directly in front of him.

The woman's mouth opened up and blood began to pour out. The man was so frightened that he wet himself. The woman uttered the words as blood kept coming out of her mouth. "He's coming…"

Suddenly the woman's body collapsed down onto the floor and she was lifeless once more. The man ran for his life.

The next morning, April was leaving to work and her sister was asleep on the couch. Trinity and Messiah and Chaos were already gone. Darkside was asleep on the floor. As April walked out the door, she got in the car and was driving to work. While she was at work, there was a woman that came up to her to make a deposit. The woman looked like she was in a panic. She asked the woman, "Is everything okay?"

The woman replied to her very quietly, "I don't know... I've been hearing strange noises in my home."

April asked her, "What do you mean?"

The woman replied, "I've been hearing all of these strange noises." The woman walked away as soon as she got her receipt.

As April stood there at the counter, she wondered to herself if the woman was experiencing the same thing her sister was experiencing. A man walked into the bank.

He walked up to the teller next to April. The teller said to the man, "How are you doing today, sir?"

He replied to him, "Doing just well."

The teller asked the man, "What can I do for you today?"

The man replied, "I'm here to make a withdrawal."

The teller said, "Okay, checking or savings?"

The man said, "Checking."

"Okay, can I get your account number?" The teller asked.

"Let me get my checkbook. I don't have it memorized." The man said. He pulled out a nine-millimeter pistol and pointed it at the teller. The man yelled out, "As you all know, I'm here to rob the bank! It should be pretty obvious so you know what comes next. Open the registers, open the vault and give me all your money. Nobody try to be a hero, or young Matthew here is gonna get a bullet between the eyes." Everyone in the bank was frozen in fear. The man yelled out, "What the hell are you waiting for??? Did I stutter? Get moving!"

All of the tellers started emptying out the registers. Two more men entered the bank. Just like their heist before, one went with the security guard to the vault, another watched the people. The man yelled out, "Everybody get down on the ground except for the tellers. You guys keep doing what I told you." The man pressed the gun to the teller's head. "Last time I robbed a bank there was a pretty woman that tried to call the cops by tripping a silent alarm. You're not gonna be as stupid as her now are you, Matthew?"

The teller replied, "No sir."

The man said, "Smart choice. I'm pretty sure you're a family man, right? Wife, kids, the whole nine yards, nice little home, little picket fence, you probably go to church regularly huh? Every Sunday?"

The teller stammered, "Yes sir," in fear.

The robber told the teller, "I bet you pray to God that everything works out fine and that your family is always safe and that's what you pray about, right Matthew?"

"Yes sir." The teller said. The robber smiled.

Soon enough the man walked out of the vault with the guard. He had a duffel bag full of money. The man holding the teller up said, "Thank you. Looks like all of your praying paid off because you get to live today."

The three men quickly exited the bank. They got into a white van and drove off. One of the robbers said, "That was great, we got another big score!"

The robber who was their leader said, "No... This was just small potatoes. It's time for us to take this to a whole new level. We're gonna run this city. And then we're gonna run MORE cities! I'm planning on building an empire, boys. Robbing banks, that's just little stuff."

Soon enough the cops all came to the bank and were questioning everyone on what happened. Finally everybody was free to leave. April went home. Everyone gathered around the kitchen table except for Darkside, who was asleep on the floor still.

April asked, "He's STILL sleeping???"

Jasmine said, "I haven't seen him move at all. I almost thought he was dead until he started snoring."

April said, "There was a robbery today. A man came in with two other guys. They robbed us and got away."

Jasmine replied, "That's horrible!"

Chaos asked, "That's terrible. Do you want me to keep an eye on the bank?"

April replied, "No, I don't think it will happen again."

Finally Darkside had woken up and walked into the kitchen and asked, "Hey guys, how is everything?"

Jasmine said, "Well look who's awake."

Darkside replied, "I was just taking a nap."

"A nap?" Jasmine asked. "I think you've been asleep since last night!"

He said, "What? I've gotta have my nap time."

April just rolled her eyes. She then said, "Today before we got robbed there was a woman who came in and she looked frightened. She told me she had been hearing noises in her house. I think she was going through the same thing Jasmine was."

Chaos then said, "Sounds like something is coming."

Messiah said, "We should probably get ready. It sounds like something catastrophic is coming."

Darkside cut in and said, "Yeah, it's probably bad but nothing we can't handle."

"After seeing your brother in action all these times, considering he doesn't even do any training, I think we are pretty safe." Trinity said.

April then put her hand on Darkside's hand and said, "I know. He protected us at Jasmine's house when all those ghosts were around."

Darkside said, "Naw, just helping a friend out. No big deal." He then stretched and said, "Well I'm gonna go take a nap."

April said, "You're going to go back to sleep? Didn't you just wake up?"

Darkside said, "Yeah, besides dinner's not even ready yet. I could get a good thirty minutes in."

April smiled at him and then Darkside walked back into the living room. With a look of disgust on her face, Trinity gave April a dirty look. April noticed this look from Trinity and turned away.

CHAPTER 9:

THE PLAN UNFOLDS

It was Saturday night. April, her sister, Darkside, and the others were all going out for a night on the town. They went to a club. They went inside and sat down at a table. The waitress brought a round of shots to the table. The group each grabbed one and drank it. Chaos then said, "Wow that was really good! What was that?"

Jasmine replied, "It's whiskey."

Chaos said, "Let's get another."

"Great!" The waitress said. "I'll get you another round."

The waitress came back with another of shots. The group took the shots together and two other ladies came up to the table. One of them said, "Hey April! Hey Jasmine. Didn't know you guys were coming out tonight!"

April replied, "Yeah, had to get out of the house."

The two ladies introduced themselves. "Hi, I'm Mindy."

The other lady introduced herself as Jessica. The others all shook hands and said hello to the two women.

Mindy asked, "So April, who are these guys? And how come you haven't told us anything about them?"

April simply replied, "Oh they're just friends. I've been really busy. Haven't been able to do much."

Jessica cut in and said, "You didn't tell us you knew the great Michael Smith!"

Messiah then said, "Well Michael Smith was what I was going by. My real name is Messiah."

Jessica said, "That's so hot!!!" Trinity simply rolled her eyes.

Mindy said, "This place is kind of lame. There's this club on the other side of town, we should all go there."

Chaos then asked, "Do they have shots over there?"

Mindy then replied, "Oh yeah… They have shots!"

Chaos stood and said, "Well let's go!"

So everyone got up and left. Before long they made it to the club on the other side of town and went inside. They sat off to the side at a table. April said to Mindy, "You whore! You brought us to a strip club!!!"

Mindy just laughed. "Well this place is more exciting than that other place."

A waitress came over to them. "Want anything to drink?"

Chaos said, "Could we get some whiskey? But instead of these shots, can we have the bottle?"

"You want the bottle?" The waitress asked in surprise.

"Yeah. These shots aren't that exciting. We want a whole bottle."

"Looks like somebody's running a tab!" The waitress said.

Chaos said, "Well I have cash, does that work?" He took out his wallet and gave the waitress a hundred dollar bill and told her to keep the change or whatever was left after paying for the bottle.

The waitress left and came back with a bottle of whiskey. As the waitress walked off again, she walked by one of the strippers and whispered in her ear, "High roller at table six."

Chaos opened the bottle and started to chug the alcohol. He drank the entire bottle in one sitting.

Mindy then said, "Wow he can really hold his liquor!"

"This is easy!" Chaos said. "I don't know how you people get drunk and sick off of this stuff. I could drink all night!"

As the group was at the table enjoying themselves, there was a man next to the stage. He was an older gentleman. The stripper walked up to him and said, "Hey sweetie!" The man seemed to be mesmerized by her.

He said, "I'm glad that you're back!"

"Me too!" She said. "You wanna take this behind closed doors?"

The man willing exclaimed, "Yes!" She got offstage, grabbed him by his tie and walked him to the back.

The two went to a backroom and sat down on a couch. She climbed on top of him. The man was very excited. The woman said, "The vacation was great. Thanks for paying for it!"

"No problem!" The old man said.

The woman said, "I would like to go shopping tomorrow, would you like to take me?"

The man said, "Yes... My wife will be at work tomorrow, I'm sure she wouldn't mind me taking you shopping."

The woman then said as she rubbed the man's head between her breasts, "I know how your wife ignores you, but I won't ignore you."

Suddenly the woman yelled out in pain and was clutching her head. The man asked, "What's wrong?"

She fell to the floor in pain. The man was in a hysterical panic and did not know what to do. As the woman was in pain, a piece of metal fell out of her head as she lay on the floor. She sat up and saw the metal as the pain went away. The shard of metal rose into the air and as it dripped with her blood, it took off and broke straight through the wall and was gone.

Back in California, a massive earthquake broke out. People were panicked again. It was the second earthquake in less than a month. While people were in their panic, the earthquake stopped, but not before ripping a six-mile hole right through Los Angeles. It began to rain.

The next day, everyone was back at April's place. April and Chaos were in the kitchen. April asked Chaos, "Chaos, can I ask you a question?"

He replied, "Sure."

She said, "I don't think Trinity likes me very much."

"No? What are you talking about?" Chaos asked.

She replied, "It's just that sometimes when all of us are hanging out, it seems like she doesn't like me. Just the other day when we were in the kitchen and I was talking to your brother she gave me a dirty look."

Chaos said, "Well Trinity has always liked my brother. But he doesn't look at her the same way."

April asked, "What do you mean? If he doesn't like her why doesn't she move on?"

"The truth is…" He said, "…A long time ago when we were all young, Trinity was out with her brother. They were playing out in an area just like the 'parks' here on Earth, and Messiah was running around playing while Trinity was by herself. As you had seen when you went to visit our home with my brother, it's not like here. We have visits from planets all around. Even though our planet is a place of peace, not everyone who comes there is peaceful. As Trinity was off by herself, there was a man from another planet that was being transported. He was about to face the judges in a trial for all of the murders he had committed throughout the universe. This creature had broken free and was on the run. He was a very powerful monster. He was over six-feet tall and had the body of what you guys call 'gorillas' here. He ran through the area and ran into Trinity.

"The monster threatened her and she was so scared. Me and my brother were walking through. We saw her and my brother ran over there. The monster was about to attack her and Darkside dove, tackling him to the ground. The security guards in the area finally found him and they took him away. Ever since then she's always had feelings for my brother. Ironically they live right down the area from us. All four of us became friends and we grew up together. We've been close ever since."

April said, "Wow… I guess I can see why she gets mad. She really does care for him."

As the others were in the living room and April and Chaos were in the kitchen making breakfast, a news story broke on the television. The reporter was talking about the massive earthquake in California the previous night. Darkside said, "Another earthquake over there? That's nuts!"

Messiah replied, "Yeah. It seems like there's been a lot of disasters happening lately. I think we might need to keep our eyes open. There have been a LOT of weird things going on."

As all of this was going on, back in Seattle there was a press conference going on about the new drug,

Lifeline. Arthur walked out in front of everybody. He said, "Good morning, ladies and gentlemen. As you all know we are all here today to talk about Lifeline. As we had mentioned before in the last press conference, Lifeline will help people everywhere. And just to be sure I want to reiterate that we are not here to play God, we just want to make life better. Now are there any question?"

A man in the audience spoke up and said, "So Mr. Quebec, have you tried Lifeline for yourself on any injuries?"

Arthur replied, "No, I have never had any injuries in a while. I'm very healthy and very lucky. Are there any more questions?"

As many others continued to raise their hands and ask questions, Crystal was sitting off to the side with a smile on her face. She was just staring at Arthur. Soon enough the press conference was over. Arthur and Crystal were in the back.

Arthur said to Crystal, "Hey thanks for being very understanding."

She replied, "It's okay, you didn't really love me. You just needed my help. No worries, it's all in the past."

"You really are the best. I don't deserve you. One day I'm sure you'll find the right man."

She smiled and said, "I know." And then she walked off.

Later that night, Arthur was in his house with the woman that he was seeing while he was with Crystal. They were on the couch and the woman appeared to be very aroused. She climbed on top of him and he was just as excited as she was. As she slowly started undressing him starting with his tie, there was a knock on the door. Arthur said, "Just ignore it. Keep going, keep going. Don't stop!"

The woman began to unbutton his shirt. There was a knock at the door again. Arthur repeated the order to ignore the knock. The knocking continued. The woman said, "Maybe we should answer it?"

He said, "No, they can wait."

She smiled. She took off her shirt and unbuttoned her bra and removed it. As Arthur smiled, she started undoing his pants. The knocking finally stopped. Arthur said, "About time… I thought they'd never go away."

She got up off of him and pulled his pants off. She then climbed back on top of him and they began kissing each other. As the two continued grabbing at each other passionately, the front door was blown straight off the hinges. The two jumped off the couch to see what was going on. It was Crystal. She walked in and was wearing a wedding dress.

Arthur yelled, "Crystal what are you doing here!? I thought you were flying back to California!"

"I am." Crystal replied. "But I wanted to stop and see you before I left."

The woman said, "Don't you get it, Crystal? Arthur doesn't want anything to do with you. He just works with you. It's me that he wants." She grabbed her breasts and held them out firmly as she ended her sentence.

Crystal walked up to them with a smile on her face. The woman said as she continued to massage her own breasts, "Did you wanna come get in on the action?" She laughed.

Crystal smiled and then grabbed her by the neck and started to choke her. Arthur said, "What are you doing!?" Crystal didn't reply, but continued to smile. She then lifted the woman off the couch and threw her into the wall. As the woman was on the floor half naked trying to crawl away, Crystal walked over to her and put her foot on the woman's neck.

"You're not going anywhere." Crystal said.

Arthur stood up and yelled at Crystal, "Stop! Please! Leave Amanda alone!"

Crystal looked back at him and then began to laugh. As Crystal had her foot on Amanda's neck she started pressing down. The woman's neck was crushed under Crystal's foot. She laid there lifeless and blood flowed out of her mouth.

Arthur yelled out, "What have you done? You crazy bitch! You're gonna pay for this! You're gonna be locked up! You're never gonna see the light of day, you psycho!"

Crystal then took her foot off Amanda's neck and began walking towards Arthur. She walked up to him with a smile on her face and punched him right in the gut, dropping Arthur to his knees in pain. As she stood in front of him, she picked him back up and he yelled out, "You crazy bitch! What's wrong with you...?" She kneed him in the groin. He fell over to his knees once again.

Arthur then tried to crawl away. She walked behind him as he was crawling. He crawled into the kitchen. She taunted him, saying, "You're not going anywhere, sweetie." She stood him up. As she was picking him up she pushed him into the wall with such force that it cracked and his body was indented into the wall. Arthur screamed out in pain. Crystal walked over to the counter, up to a knife set and pulled out one of the knives and threw it directly at Arthur. The knife hit Arthur right in the stomach and blood flowed out of the wound.

She picked up another knife and threw it at him, this time the knife hit him in his left shoulder. She picked up another knife and threw it again, this one hit him in the throat. She grabbed yet another knife and it hit him dead center in the chest.

She then walked over to him. She pulled the knife in his chest out and blood spurted out. She took the knife and made a large cut across the right side of his face. Crystal was smiling the entire time. She then said, "You see this, Arthur? This is my mother's wedding dress. She gave this to me to wear on the day that I got married. I thought you cared about me. You said you loved me, but you lied to me just like everybody else did. I'm tired of men breaking my heart.

You chose that whore in the living room over me? I hope it was worth it." She stabbed him in the chest right next to where his heart was and then used her left hand to dig straight through his chest. She said, "Oh, your heart's beating fast! Are you scared? It's okay, it's almost over."

With a look of horror on his face, his eyes were open wide. She then ripped his heart right out of his chest.

Arthur died. As Crystal held his heart in her hand, she walked over and sat it on the counter. She was covered in blood. She took the knife that she was holding in her other hand, and stabbed it right through the heart. She looked over at Arthur one last time, examining his body still stuck in the wall. She looked over at the dead woman in the living room with a crushed throat.

She then started to laugh and what seemed to be tears of joy ran down her face. As she was covered in blood and the mascara ran down her eyes with the tears, she walked out of Arthur's house and left.

CHAPTER 10:

BEGINNING OF THE END

There was a press conference that the President of the United States was holding. A lot of people were anticipating what the President had to say. The president walked onstage. He approached the podium and began to speak.

"As all of you know, there have been a number of natural disasters in the last month, ranging from hurricanes to earthquakes, hailstorms, blizzards, and not just here in our great nation, but all over the world. It was reported just last night that right outside of Japan all of the water froze. I know there have been a lot of people saying this is an act of God, some may even say that it's just an imbalance but whatever the case may be I want the American people to be ready for it. We already have shelters being put up in every state. I've spoken with all military branches to be prepared for what may come."

A man in the audience rose and said, "President Gutierrez, how ready do you think we can be to face these disasters that are taking place? After all, the shelters… can they really hold everyone?"

The president replied, "We are doing our best to construct adequate shelters and we will construct more if needed. We will do what it takes to protect the people of this nation."

A man quickly ran out onstage and whispered something in the president's ear. President Gutierrez then said, "My apologies, there is an urgent situation I need to address. It's an emergency." The president walked off the stage. The crowd was in chatter, wondering what was going on.

Back at April's place, the gang was hanging out. They were watching TV in the living room. Breaking news interrupted their program. The tide was raising right outside of California and water was pouring onto the land. The news reporter spoke out saying that if this continued, the state of California would be underwater.

April said, "I wonder if this has anything to do with all of the strange events that have been happening."

Chaos asked, "What do you mean?"

Just think about it." She said. "The natural disasters, people talking about hearing things in the night, all of these church people saying the end is near…"

Chaos then said, "You're probably right. It could be a coincidence but it is pretty strange."

As all of this was going on, downtown in Seattle Crystal Jones drove up in a black truck. She got out and grabbed a backpack. There were a couple of men standing outside of a building. They stared and one of them whistled at her. She gave the man a dirty look. The man winked at her and said, "Hey sexy!"

Crystal was dressed in an all-black outfit. She had black boots with black leather pants and a matching leather top without any sleeves. She then turned and walked into the building. The men yelled out, "Where are you goin', pretty lady?"

She entered the building, a radio station, and got into the elevator. She went to the top floor of this building. As she walked down the hall she went to the exit door to go onto the roof. There was a security guard who asked, "What can I help you with ma'am?"

She yelled at the guard to get out of her way. The guard replied, "I'm sorry but you can't have access to the roof. Staff and technical teams only. Do you have a badge?"

Crystal repeated to the man aggressively, "Get out of the way."

"No badge, no access." The guard said.

She then kicked him right between the legs and the man dropped to his knees. He said, "You crazy bitch! What's wrong with you?"

She then took both of her hands, twisted his head around all the way and snapped his neck. His body fell over and Crystal passed him to walk onto the roof. She walked towards the satellite on top of the building. She then took off the backpack, opened it up, and took out two boxes. One of them had wires dangling from it. She hooked it up to the satellite system. The second box was opened up. She took out a chip, then inserted it into the first box. She returned to the bag and pulled out a camera. It was set up on a tripod and she plugged it into the box. She flipped the switch on the box and then turned on the camera.

All across the world, televisions everywhere now broadcasting what was on the camera that Crystal set up. People worldwide were shocked. Crystal walked in front of the camera. She introduced herself. "I am Crystal Jones." She then said, "Good afternoon everyone. I'm here to tell you all about a new future. A future where there will be no more mistreatment of women... a future where man will no longer screw things up. That's the problem with society today. It's ran by men. The problem with everything is all because of a man. Men say they know what they want, but they don't. They act like they know what's best, but they don't. And I'm here to change all of that. A new world where women are in control and men will take their place underneath a woman, how it should be. A world where a man's only purpose is to serve a woman. Here in moments, I will give women everywhere the world that they deserve."

There was a man and his wife that were in an electronics store looking at TVs when this broadcast came on. He looked at his wife and said, "Who is this crazy woman?"

His wife replied, "I don't know."

Back on top of the roof of the radio station, Crystal walked away from the camera and to the box that was connected to the satellite dish. She flipped another switch. Suddenly there was a loud screeching noise. Every TV and radio station was filled with static. High above the Earth, every single satellite that orbited the Earth was receiving a signal. The screeching sound and signal finally stopped. Crystal walked back in front of the camera. It was transmitting again. She spoke once more, saying, "It is done. The fall of man begins now…"

Suddenly women everywhere were somehow becoming hypnotized. Back in the electronics store, the same couple who had commented on Crystal, the woman became entranced. The man asked his wife, "Honey what's wrong?"

She then looked at him and said very angrily, "Get on your knees!"

He looked at his wife in confusion at his wife and said, "What?" She repeated for him to get on his knees. He looked at his wife with a weird look. "What are you talking about? Why should I get on my knees?"

She then kicked him between the legs, dropping him to his knees. As the man was writhing in pain, many other women in the store were entranced as well and began attacking nearby men. There was a man walking down the street with his girlfriend.

His girlfriend suddenly started yelling at him with a crazed look in her eye, she said, "Bow down, you piece of trash!"

The man looked at his girlfriend and cried out, "What did you say?"

"You heard me." She said. "Bow down to me, you worthless piece of trash." The woman rose her hand and slapped the man hard. He just stood there with a look of absolute confusion on his face.

"What was that for???" He demanded. She tried to swing again but this time he caught her hand. He asked her, "What's wrong with you?" This man was about six-feet tall and very muscular. His girlfriend then grabbed him by the neck and choked him. He tried to break the hold but couldn't do it. His girlfriend seemed to be super-strong.

Crystal then said in front of the camera, "Any man that does not want to take his rightful place at a woman's feet will be executed." She then walked over to the edge of the building. As she looked down at the streets below she saw the madness taking place with women taking control over men.

Meanwhile back at April's place, April and her sister began yelling at Darkside, Chaos and Messiah. April walked up to Chaos and slapped him in the face. With a look of confusion on his face, he stood there puzzled. She slapped him once more and then pointed at the ground by her side. Jasmine then said, "What are you stupid? Do as she says and kneel before your goddess."

Darkside both looked at each other, confused. Jasmine then said, "You two worms join him! All three of you bow down right now!" The three of them looked at each other. They didn't know what was going on. Jasmine walked up to Darkside and grabbed him by the throat. She looked into his eyes and said, "You worthless man! You're nothing but a waste of space. Trash that should be thrown away."

In complete confusion, Darkside asked Jasmine, "Is it that time of the month? Did we do something wrong?"

With her hand around his neck, she yelled at him one more time, "Get down on the ground!"

Trinity then walked inside from the back yard. She asked, "What's going on?"

Trinity looked at all of the women with an equally confused look on her face as the men had. Darkside said, "I don't know but for some reason April and Jasmine are mad and being really rude!"

Trinity yelled out, "Take your hand off of Darkside!!!"

April looked over at Trinity and said, "What's wrong? You know they are all nothing but garbage! You know their place is on the floor!"

Trinity asked, "What's wrong with you? What are you going on about?"

April then said, "It's the dawn of a new world! A world where men take their place beneath a woman where they belong."

Darkside then scratched his head and said, "I thought this place was an equal, free planet. I don't understand what you mean." Darkside then pulled Jasmine's hand away from his throat easily. Jasmine threw a right punch straight at Darkside but he caught it.

Trinity walked over to Jasmine and yelled, "If you ever put your hands on him again I'll make sure you never walk again!"

April then said, "You would betray your own kind for these men?"

Chaos said, "Something's not right! I know April and her sister would never act this way. Something's wrong!"

"There's nothing wrong, these two are just crazy!!!" Trinity said.

Darkside agreed. "We had better get out of here and find out what's going on."

The four of them left April's house. As April left she yelled out, "You will all see! Even you, you traitor!"

As the group walked down the streets they saw people fighting everywhere. Men were being forced to bow down to their female counterparts.

As the four of them continued to walk down the street, they saw a store with TVs in the window. Crystal Jones was on every screen, saying, "The world is as it should be. The world will be controlled by a woman."

Chaos looked at his brother and said, "I bet you she's the one behind this!"

"I think you're right, brother." Darkside said. "Let's go find her."

Messiah then said, "We don't even know where she's at!"

Trinity said, "I know where she's at. A few weeks ago there was a press conference where she and some guy were talking about a new drug. I bet you she's over there where it was being held, over in Washington."

The three of them took off running. They moved so quickly that within five minutes they were in Washington. As they arrived in Washington it was a madhouse there just the same as it was in New Mexico. While they continued walking around looking for Crystal they didn't see her anywhere in sight. Crystal herself was now walking around, indulging in the sights of what was going on.

As she was relishing in the new world she had created, she ran into Darkside and the others. Crystal called out to Trinity. "What are you doing? Why aren't these men in their place?"

Trinity replied back, "So *you're* the crazy bitch that's doing all of this!"

With a crazed look on her face, Crystal said, "What's wrong? Don't you like the new world?"

Trinity said, "This is crazy. What you're doing is wrong."

Darkside asked, "How did you make all of these women turn?"

Crystal replied, "It was simple. I hooked up a machine that transmitted a signal to all of the satellites orbiting the Earth. The signal is then broadcast here and takes control of women. It's only a matter of time before the signal takes full effect and women are in the same mindset I am."

Chaos yelled, "You're crazy! You've lost your mind! This is supposed to be the land of the free!"

"Shut your mouth! The reason the world is the way it is is because it's not being run right." Crystal said. "War all the time, global hunger, so much hatred and anger. And who's been running the world? All of these leaders who say they know what's best are men. The truth is they don't know what's best. They just think they do. They're blinded by their male pride, too stubborn to admit that they don't know what's best and that they are wrong."

Darkside then said, "What you're doing is wrong, and we will stop you!"

Crystal laughed madly. "For whatever reason" Crystal said, "I don't know why SHE isn't taking her place with the rest of the women, but has decided to ally herself with worthless garbage. No matter, all three of you men will die and she will be killed as well for betraying her kind."

CHAPTER 11:

MAN VS WOMAN

As the four of them stood there staring at Crystal, Darkside looked at his friends and said, "Guys, I got this."

Trinity then said, "You're going to go fight her all by yourself?"

"Well… yeah?" Darkside said. "It shouldn't take too long to beat her."

Trinity said, "To be honest with you I'd like to take a crack at her…"

Darkside said, "No. If I can't beat her, I'll let you guys step in." Darkside then walked away from the group and started for Crystal.

As the two stared in each other's eyes, Crystal said, "So you're the first one that's gonna die." Darkside stood there and didn't say a word. Crystal then spoke again. "You're worthless. Nothing. A nobody. You're breathing air that you do not deserve." Darkside continued to stand there, not saying a word.

Trinity yelled out, "What are you waiting for? Bash her face in!"

Crystal yelled out, "I'll deal with you later!" Crystal then threw a right hook hitting Darkside right in the face. He didn't budge and still stood there, stiff as statue. Crystal laughed and said, "I see that you're stronger than the average man! No matter, you will still die."

Crystal then grabbed Darkside by the neck. She started pushing him back. He braced himself and they stopped moving. She then released her hands from his neck. She threw another punch with her right hand but Darkside caught her fist. She then leapt forward and head-butted him right in the face. Still, Darkside stood motionless. Glaring at her.

She then took a step back, leapt forward and tackled Darkside. She hit him with such force that the two of them flew back into a vehicle. She then got up, grabbed Darkside by the neck and pushed him down to the ground. She yelled at him, "Bow down, you slave!!!"

Darkside slowly got up. Crystal threw yet another right hook at Darkside but the punch had no effect on him at all. She then smiled at him. She grabbed him by his arm and flung him across the street, into a building through the wall. Just as he stood up, she came rushing for him. She tackled him into the rubble from the broken building.

She then stood up, walked over, picked up a chair and as Darkside stood up, she smashed it over his back, knocking him down to the ground again. She grabbed him by the shoulder, raised him up and hit him with a hard right uppercut. This time, he did not stand still. The punch knocked him back. Taking steps backwards she then ran towards him, leapt in the air and kicked him in the chest. The impact of the kick knocked Darkside through another wall to the outside of the building.

She approached him again, grabbed him by the ankle and began to drag him through the rubble and broken pieces of concrete. She was dragging his body and stopped, then yelled out to the others. "This is your fate! You are all going to die!" She dropped his leg and then said, "Who's ready to step up next and perish?"

Trinity then said, "I got this. I'm gonna take her out. She's gonna pay for what she did."

Crystal smiled and began walking towards them. Darkside called out, "Where are you going? You still haven't beat me yet! To be honest, if that's the best you've got you might as well quit because you're not gonna win." Crystal froze in her tracks and turned around abruptly.

"You just got beat down and now you're talking like you're going to win? I must have banged your head too hard on the pavement!" Crystal said.

Darkside stood up. He walked back over to her. Crystal said, "Your friends are lucky; they get to live a little bit longer. It's going to take a bit more to kill you."

She then took off running straight for Darkside. He side-stepped her, and quickly followed with a right hook, punching her in the side of the head. She began to stumble a bit off balance and he rushed over, grabbed her and jumped into the air. Her arms were pinned to her sides as he held her tight. He then let her go. While she fell back towards the ground, he dove back down to the ground. He dove so fast that he passed her and landed on his feet. Just as she was about to hit the ground, he leapt up and tackled his shoulder into her back. Crystal's body fell and hit the ground. Darkside landed on his feet once again.

Darkside walked over to her body. But before he could grab her, she lifted her right leg and kicked him in the stomach. When he leaned forward she used the same leg to kick him in the side of the face. As Darkside was off-balance from the kick, she quickly got up and kneed him in the face. Darkside's head whipped back violently.

While he tried to regain his balance, she ran and jumped on top of him, knocking him down to the ground. She put both hands on his face and repeatedly lifted and smashed his face into the ground. After a while she stopped and stood up, then looked down at Darkside. She put her right foot right on his neck and said, "It's time for you to die."

CHAPTER 12:

CRYSTAL'S PAST

As Crystal had her foot on Darkside's neck, Crystal said, "My whole life I've been screwed over by a man. I've seen other women screwed over by men. Ever since I was a little girl, I've been hurt by a man. I was just a young girl in junior high. There was a boy in Junior High that I was dating. He said he loved me. He said he cared about me, but he didn't. It happened time and time again. I remember my sophomore year of high school, there was a boy that I was dating. He too said that he would always be there and that he loved me. But what did he do? He dumped me for another girl. Then again in my senior year in high school, I was getting ready for my prom. Completely dressed up, I went to my prom and what happened? The boy that I was dating dumped me right there and left with another girl and told me that he never loved me. He said that it was just a joke that everyone wanted to see. I cried myself to sleep on that night.

"Even later on when I was in college, I was dating Jacob. Just like the others before, he said that he cared about me and we would graduate and be together. But he did as the others before him had done: He broke my heart and ran away with the girl I thought was my best friend. Then I remember going home to visit one year in college. It was the holiday season…

My mother had found out that my father had an affair and was sleeping with another woman. My mom was devastated and so was I. Later on, my senior year I would go to a party and get drugged and raped by four of the members of the football team. And of course, nothing happened to them because they were star players on that team. Justice was never served.

"After I got out of college I met another man who would feed me the same lies all of those other men did. He said that he loved me and cared about me. But it was just a lie. He, too, broke my heart. I came home and saw him packing his bags. I thought he really cared because we lived together, but he told me that he had enough and that he was leaving.

Then there was my colleague, Arthur Quebec. Longest relationship I've ever had. Two years of lies… And what happened? I went out and bought lingerie for him. And of course I come back to his room and he's with another woman. He never cared about me. He was only using me to help him work on his Lifeline project. My whole life I was hurt by men and I'm sick of it. I made an example out of Arthur. I went to his house, and I killed the bimbo that he was caught with, and I ripped out his heart for breaking mine."

Trinity looked over at Chaos and said, "Wow, no wonder she's nuts."

Chaos then said, "She has had a hell of a past, but regardless her actions are still wrong."

As Crystal continued to look down at Darkside with her foot on his throat, she said, "This is why I did what I did. Men are the problem and they need to be put in their place. Just as you are. You're nothing but dirt underneath my feet." Crystal then lifted her foot off of Darkside's throat and just as she was about to stomp on his neck and break it, he caught her foot.

 Crystal was shocked. Darkside looked up at her and said, "You were hurt in the past, but that does not give you the right to do what you've done. What you're doing is madness and it's uncalled for."

"You're wrong, men are the problem! Men deserve to be slaves!" Crystal argued. "For years they've treated women as second-class citizens and put them beneath them. They know that women are superior and that's why they've done this for so many years."

Your taking your unhappiness out men. Sure those guys did you wrong, but what you are doing is just down right madness. I won't allow you to do this. He said to her.

With a look of anger on her face she tried to force her foot down onto him, but wasn't able to do so. Darkside then push her foot up and rolled away. Jumping back to his feet, he told her, "You should really think your actions." Shut up she yelled! She then took off running at him and was about to tackle him. In a blink of an eye, Trinity step in between Crystal and Darkside.

Get out of the way Crystal yelled! I'm done listening to you talk. Trinity replied. I'll take it from Darkside, you can sit this one out. I can't let you have all the fun now. I'm gonna teach this nut job a lesson! Crystal started to laughing, your gonna teach me a lesson? She said.

"Your out of your mind you dumb confused whore!" I will kill you then destroy him, and any other man that has a problem. What I say is law!

Trinity looked over at Darkside, he just nodded his head and then walked to the side where his brother and Messiah was at. Crystal and Trinity stood still. As the other on the side was watching the two of them, Crystal slowly started to walk up to Trinity. Now standing face to face, Crystal cane out with a right hook punch, but Trinity knocked it away. Crystal then came with a left jab, but Trinity knocked it away as well. The girls tied up. It seemed that they was both on the same level, as neither of the two was moving an inch.

Trinity smiled, and hit her with a high knee to gut. As the tie up hold was broken, Trinity came out with left and right jabs, that was hitting Crystal right between the eyes. As Crystal continued to take the punches, she stared to fall back. Trinity then hit her with a right kick to the ribs. Crystal was reeling from the hits but now started to laugh. Now looking back at Trinity as she continued to laugh.

"Your one crazy case" Trinity said. Crystal finally stopped laughing and drove at her. The two of them was now exchanging punches.

As the two of them continued to exchange punches as Darkside, Chaos and Messiah looked on, Crystal had a smile on her face as if she were amused by the battle. Trinity yelled out to her, "You think this is funny?"

She replied back to her, "I think it's funny how you're fighting for the wrong team, I think it's funny that you think you're gonna win, I think it's funny that you're already dead."

Trinity replied, "I've had enough of your mouth." Crystal continued to throw punches, Trinity started blocking them one by one. Crystal took a step back to put distance between herself and Trinity.

With a smile on her face, Crystal said, "Not bad! You've got some moves. But you're still going to die." Crystal then leapt at Trinity and in a split moment Trinity side-stepped to the left and elbowed Crystal in the back of the head, knocking her to the ground. Trinity then walked over to Crystal and looked down on her. Crystal laughed as if she was amused.

As Darkside and the others watched in the distance, Chaos said, "That's one crazy lady!"

Darkside replied, "Given her history, I can understand why she's nuts. But it still doesn't give her the right to do what she's done."

"That's true." Chaos said. "Do you think Trinity can beat her?"

"I have no doubt that Trinity will do well, but I don't know if she can beat her. There's something about Crystal." Darkside said.

"What do you mean, brother?" Chaos asked.

"Just look at it." Darkside said. "Crystal Jones is from Earth, just a normal person and yet she has incredible strength and abilities as if she wasn't from here. People from this planet aren't that strong. She did something to herself to become that way."

Chaos replied, "Well that's true brother, but even though she's made herself stronger with these abilities, I don't see how she can fight toe to toe with one of us."

"You would think, Chaos, that there's something different about her. She's fighting with rage, wanting revenge. She's been wronged too many times and she's fighting for revenge." Darkside said. "Her emotions are only of rage. She might as well have a heart of stone."

As the fight continued between Trinity and Crystal, Trinity grabbed Crystal and got her in a rear choke hold. Trinity yelled out, "How about you just give up?" Crystal didn't say a word. She then leapt into the air as Trinity held onto her. As they rose into the air, Crystal maneuvered to her side and elbowed Trinity in her side until she had broken the hold and got out. Trinity threw a right punch but Crystal ducked and came back with a right high kick straight to the head.

Trinity was a bit disoriented from the hit. Crystal dove at her, tackling her all the way back to the ground. Crystal stood up, picking up Trinity and kneed her directly in the face. Trinity fell over to the ground. Crystal said, "Look what this has got you! You wanna side with these men? Now it's just gonna lead to your death!" Crystal walked over and grabbed Trinity by the throat and picked her up midway, then started to choke her. Crystal then lifted up her left hand and said, "This is it! Your final moment!" Trinity looked up at Crystal. Trinity then pointed her right hand at Crystal's face.

Trinity's hand began to glow with a purple light and crystal paused in surprise. "What the…?" She exclaimed. Suddenly it started getting very windy. There must have been fifty-mile per hour winds on the street. Crystal yelled out, "What are you doing?" The wind began to get stronger and stronger and gashes began to appear on Crystal's arms. Crystal yelled out, "You bitch! What are you doing? Look what you've done!" The gashes continued to appear on Crystal's arms and then a gash on the back of her neck, on the lower left side of her face, and her forehead.

Crystal released the hold from Trinity's neck. Trinity stood up and said, "It's the winds of change. And things are changing right now! It's you who is in their final moments."

Crystal yelled out in pain, "I can't believe what's going on!"

Trinity said, "Believe it, because it's happening."

Crystal was in excruciating pain with the gashes all over her body and the wind continued to blow at an outrageous speed. Crystal said, "I can't believe this!!! I can't believe it!!! You think I'm done!!!"

With a shocked look on her face, Trinity looked on as Crystal leapt up and smacked her with a punch that landed right between the eyes. The moment that Crystal's fist connected with Trinity's face, the wind instantly went away. Trinity just stood there, frozen like a statue. Crystal pulled back her fist and the wounds all over her body healed instantly.

Trinity, standing there stiff as a statue, fell down to the ground. Crystal then looked back at Darkside and the others. Messiah and Chaos were in shock. Darkside, with a serious look on his face, said, "I'll take it from here. Messiah, go get your sister."

Chaos put his hand on Darkside's shoulder and said, "No, brother." Darkside paused for the moment and looked back at him. Chaos said, "Did you just see what she did to Trinity? Do you think it's a good idea for you to go and fight her by yourself? We should fight her together."

Darkside said, "No, let me fight her."

Crystal yelled out to the both of them, "It doesn't matter who fights me. You're both gonna die. In fact I haven't had a shot with him. I already know I can beat you."

Darkside looked at Chaos and said, "Well Major, would you like a shot at her by yourself? It seems she's calling you out." Chaos was silent for the moment as he seemed to be collecting his thoughts.

Crystal yelled again, "What's wrong? Are you scared? You're gonna die either way! Do you wanna die now, or later on?"

Chaos replied, "I'm not gonna die, you are. I've got this one, brother. You can sit this one out."

Darkside said, "Oh well."

Chaos walked over to Crystal and stood face-to-face with her. Messiah came over and picked up his sister. As he was carrying Trinity off from the battlefield, Crystal yelled out, "Make sure you take out the trash, that traitor of her own kind!" Crystal then turned her attention back to Chaos.

Chaos said, "You've had it easy so far. You may have been lucky but you won't have the same luck with me. My brother is too relaxed. He could have finished you off already, but I don't know why he was taking his time. You just caught Trinity by surprise. You won't have the same luck with me."

Crystal let out a laugh. She said, "So after I beat you and that other guy that carried the trash off the battlefield, he steps in to fight me? Is he gonna give me the same speech how you were holding back and how he's gonna beat me? Is that what's gonna happen next?"

"That's not gonna happen." He replied. "I'm the last person you'll be fighting."

"We'll see." She said.

CHAPTER 13:

A TEST OF STRENGTH

As Crystal and Chaos stood face-to-face not moving, staring into each other's eyes, Messiah walked over to Darkside with Trinity over his shoulder. Darkside said to him, "Get her someplace safe, far away from here. There are other women who will try to attack you, so take her to a place that's clear of people. She's going to have to recover. She's barely alive. Me and Chaos will take it from here."

Messiah then flew off with Crystal on his shoulder. Darkside continued to watch on as Chaos and Crystal continued their stare down, not saying a word. Crystal threw a right hook block but Chaos blocked it. She then threw a left hook, but he blocked it as well. She tried to throw another right hook but he blocked it another time. Crystal then threw a high kick and hit Chaos upside the head, but he didn't move an inch. Crystal lowered her leg back down and said, "Whoa, you're tougher than I thought! No matter, you're still gonna die."

As Crystal continued to ramble on about how she was going to kill him, he threw a right hook, knocking her in the left side of her head. Crystal then threw a right punch at him but he caught her fist. She was shocked. While holding her fist, he threw her back into a streetlight. The light post was indented into the shape of Crystal's body as she made contact with it. Chaos then walked over to her. She looked up at him. "Is this the best you got?" She asked. He didn't say a word. With a show of disrespect she spat right in Chaos's face. She began to laugh. A look of anger emerged on Chaos's face.

Chaos tackled her and grabbed onto her legs, driving his shoulder into her stomach. He began to yell as he kept running with her, holding onto her. There was a row of light posts down the street and he ran her through each one. After running four blocks of light posts, he stopped and slammed her onto the pavement. He walked over to her and knelt down by her side, put his hand on her neck and lifted her up. He slammed her into the ground, lifted her up, and slammed her into the ground again. He removed his hand from her neck. Crystal started to laugh. As she was laughing, Chaos slapped her across the face. He then took his right hand and took her by the throat, and stood up.

He started walking very slowly, dragging her. He lifted her up into a standing position, then came in close and kneed her straight in the gut. As she leaned over forward in pain, Chaos then dropped an elbow on her upper back.

As Crystal was in pain from the hits she was taking, Chaos let go of her and dropped her to the ground. Focused on the situation at hand as he stared at her, she slowly started to move and stand back up. He said to her, "You're strong but you're at a disadvantage. You can heal rapidly but it won't be enough to save you. My brother may have taken it easy on you, but I won't. Trinity was just too careless, but I won't be that way."

As she stood up and stared into Chaos's eyes there was a moment of silence. They stood in the middle of the street surrounded in the carnage that took place within the last few hours. As the madness engulfed the world and this new incarnation of slavery had come back, Darkside looked back as his brother was fighting with Crystal. Crystal boldly walked up to Chaos and stood what seemed to be an inch away from him. The two were face-to-face, not moving a muscle. A smile then came on her face, and the same as well for Chaos. Crystal slowly took a step back.

After slowly setting some distance between herself and Chaos she turned and started walking away very slowly. Chaos yelled out, "What's wrong? You decided that you can't win? You finally realized you can't win?" She continued to walk away. With a look of anger on his face Chaos approached her while she started to walk.

Darkside yelled, "Brother, look out!"

For the moment, Chaos looked back at his brother, and Crystal did a backflip and landed right in front of Chaos as he was looking back at his brother. From the moment that Crystal's feet hit the ground, Chaos came with a right elbow, knocking her off balance. "Not bad." She said.

Chaos replied, "What did you think? I was some rookie? I was the commanding major from the division that I came from!"

"Well done!" She said. She then threw a kick to his side, but he blocked it. A right hook, but he blocked it. She threw a right jab and he caught her fist. A smile emerged on Crystal's face once again. Now she started attacking him even faster, throwing lefts, rights, and kicks at will. He seemed to block every attack as they came towards him.

While the two continued, meanwhile Messiah was carrying Trinity away. He was flying up in the air carrying her over his shoulder when she started to move. Trinity woke up and asked, "What's going on?"

"You were fighting with Crystal." He said.

"I can't believe I got knocked out. I was pretty sure I had to be. I remember I was using one of my finishing attacks on her and now I just remember waking up." Trinity said.

"She hit you pretty hard." Messiah said. "After the impact of the hit, you just stood there before you fell over. I was taking you away so you could find a spot to recover."

She replied, "We have no time to recover. We have to get back to where the fight's happening! I can't believe she knocked me out. I'm not gonna stand for this. We need to go back! I just got careless."

The two of them turned around and flew back to where the battle was happening. As they were on their way, the fight continued with Chaos and Crystal. Crystal threw a right high kick for Chaos's side, but he caught it by hooking it with his arm. He then pulled her in close and his her right between the eyes. She jumped back to get some distance and he ran after her. He tackled her right into a parked car on the side of the street. He then threw a right punch directly for her. She moved and he slammed his fist against the hood of the car. He turned around, Crystal took off and started running down the street. Chaos followed her. As she was running, she jumped to the left, turned around and came around with a left hook. She hit Chaos right between the eyes but he did not move. He just stood there. He then reached forward, grabbed her by the neck and brought her in close.

He whispered into her ear, "What's wrong? Pain, torture, not any fun when you're not the one causing it? Is reality starting to set into you?"

She replied to him, "Is reality starting to set into you?" From this point as he held her by the neck, he dropped her onto her knee. As her back bent over his knee and his hand was still on her neck, she threw a kick hitting him in the head. He stayed there, in position. She repeatedly kicked him to force him to release the hold. She stood up standing right in front of him and he came at her with left and right punches. She seemed to block every hit as it came to her.

As the two continued exchanging blows and Darkside watched on, Trinity and Messiah both returned to the battlefield. Trinity said out to Darkside, "I can't believe that nutjob knocked me out. I shouldn't have been so careless. I know I can beat her."

"Don't worry about it. Don't let it get you down." Darkside said. "Like I said to my brother before, there's something different about her. She feels revenge and has something deep inside that is blinding her, a rage."

Suddenly from out of nowhere, two people descended from the sky. In shock, Darkside said, "Ojohna! What are you doing here on Earth?"

He replied out to Darkside, "I was sent by the division leaders after a meeting. They need your brother and you, if possible, to come back to the planet Ying Yang. A war has broken out and they are requesting Major Chaos to come back with us."

"A war broke out?" Darkside asked. "What happened?"

Ojohna said to him, "There's an unknown military group that has come to our planet with a list of demands. They said that if they don't give into our demands they would wage war with the planet."

Darkside replied back to him, "Man, there's just no break! Bad guys everywhere. What's up with everybody wanting to take over? I was planning on taking a nap after this business with Crystal Jones was over."

Ojohna laughed. "I can see you're still the same old Darkside that you were back home. Well the people need you and your brother, and Trinity and Messiah as well. We need to mobilize and we need all resources. They have allies, but we don't know how many. This could possibly be the biggest war we've ever fought."

Trinity then cut in and said, "We need to wrap things up here before we take off. Instead of fighting Crystal one-by-one we need to take her out. I wanted to have one more shot at her one-on-one but that isn't going to happen. We just need to get rid of her right now!"

Ojohna said, "Great! So you guys will come back with us, right?"

"Of course we will." Darkside said. "But we must finish business here first."

Trinity, Messiah, Ojohna, Darkside and Ojohna's partner all started walking towards the street where Chaos and Crystal were fighting. As Chaos and Crystal were still exchanging punches, Crystal stepped to the left. She then took a step back and said, "What's this? Now you're gonna bring your whole gang? I knew something like this would happen and I've planned for it. I have a fail-safe! If I couldn't beat you I'm going to make this world free of men!"

"What are you talking about!?" Darkside yelled.

CHAPTER 14:

TIME STRUGGLE

Crystal took off running. She ran, jumped in the air, and flew away. Darkside yelled out, "I don't know what she's planning but we need to follow her and find out fast." The entire group took off after her flying.

Crystal was flying back to the building where all of the madness had first started. She went over to the box that she had installed on the satellite. There was a bag sitting on the floor. She picked it up, pulled a small keyboard out, and plugged it into a small port on the side of the box. She started typing in a code.

The box began to make noise. Darkside and the others arrived on the rooftop where she was at. He yelled out to her, "What are you doing, Crystal?"

"I just entered in a code. This is my backup plan in case things went wrong! Every single man on this planet will become extinct!" She yelled.

"What are you talking about?" Darkside asked.

"This system I just activated will shoot another signal that will bounce off a satellite and hit every other satellite around the world. Just as I took control of all the women around the world so they would assert their dominance over their inferior counterpart, this new signal will target every single man on the face of the Earth. If it produces testosterone, it will die." Crystal said.

Chaos yelled out, "What are you, nuts?"

Crystal said, "I'm not crazy. I am just doing what should have been done. I may not win here today, but I will change everything! My goal of this planet, this world, being a female-dominant planet will come true whether I'm here to see it or not. I have multiple boxes set up everywhere and there's no way you can stop the signal before it launches. There's too many."

The group had a shocked look on their face. They didn't know what to do. Crystal started laughing though she felt she might die, she felt she had still won. Darkside then said, "Wait. It's not over yet! I have an idea. I need all of you to find all of these boxes and destroy them."

Crystal yelled out, "You're not gonna have enough time! In ten minutes from now, the signal will be complete and it will be too late. You'll never find the five boxes I've placed, there's no way."

Darkside said out to the group, "These boxes could be anywhere around the world. We have to find them. If worst comes to worst, we'll probably have to smash the satellites in space."

Crystal then picked up the camera that was hooked up to the box that made the broadcast she had sent earlier. She turned it on and said to the camera, "These men are going to try to stop us from what we are trying to accomplish. Guard these boxes and stop any man who tries to oppose us!"

Darkside said, "You guys know what to do. Find those boxes. And if need be, destroy those satellites. I'll take care of 'Crazy' over here."

Crystal started to laugh. "You're not going to make it. You've wasted too much time standing here putting your plan together!"

Darkside yelled out, ran and tackled her right off the roof of the building. The others took off in different directions to look for the boxes. As Darkside and Crystal were heading straight toward the ground, she began laughing and said, "It's too late! It's over! There's no way you're gonna win!"

The two of them hit the ground. Darkside stood up, standing right next to Crystal. "I've been holding back this whole time. I had seen some good in you, but I guess I was wrong. No more games, no holding back. It's time for you to go."

Crystal stood up and she said, "I've been holding back the entire time myself. I wanted to see how strong you and your friends are and now I can see that you do not even compare. Inferior, just like every man is."

Darkside threw a right hook and hit her right in the jaw. As Crystal's head turned from the impact of the punch, he followed around with a left uppercut to the jaw and then threw left and rights straight at her body, followed by an elbow to the side of the face.

As the fight continued between Crystal and Darkside, the others flew around the world trying to spot the box. Chaos had spotted a box on top of the Statue of Liberty's crown. He flew down to the statue and ripped the box right off the frame that it was attached to and smashed it on the ground. Trinity was flying looking for a box, and was in Egypt when she spotted one of the boxes on the tip top of a pyramid.

She ripped it off and slammed it into the side of the pyramid, smashing it. Messiah was flying through and found a box on top of the Eiffel Tower in Paris, France. He flew down and threw a punch straight to the box and the box was destroyed by impact but the tower leaned over a noticeable amount.

Messiah then looked around, and ran off before anyone could see him. Ojohna and his partner were flying around and they found the fourth box. It was sitting on top of Mount Rushmore. They flew down and Ojohna's partner ripped the box off the side of Abraham Lincoln's head and threw it into the air. Ojohna shot a laser out of his finger, blowing the box to bits.

Ojohna made the comment, "There won't be any slavery here today." Ojohna, his partner, Trinity, and Messiah all met back in downtown Seattle where Darkside was still fighting Crystal.

Each of them said, "I got a box!"

Chaos then said, "We're missing one. Where's the fifth box?"

Messiah said, "I don't know! We only have a minute and thirty seconds to get it!"

As Darkside and Crystal were continuing their battle, Chaos yelled, "We found four out of five boxes! We don't know where the last one is at!"

Darkside yelled out while fighting, "Did you guys get the main one on the top of the building?"

Chaos and the others all looked at each other. Messiah yelled out quickly, "Ok we're gonna get that one…"

As the group all flew back to the top of the building to get the final box, Crystal continued her fight with Darkside. Darkside said to her as they continued to exchange hits, "It's over! Your plan has been thwarted! There won't be any genocide today!"

When the group arrived on top of the building, Chaos walked over to the box, ripped it off and smashed it onto the ground. The box was still making noise. Messiah yelled out, "It didn't stop! It's still running!"

Ojohna said, "We're gonna have to find a way to destroy it—and fast!"

Chaos then pointed his hand directly at the box. His hand began to glow. He put his hand on the box. There was an explosion. As the smoke cleared, the box was still there. With a great look of surprise on his face, the box was still there with hardly any damage on it.

Messiah yelled out, "What are we gonna do? We're running out of time! We only have thirty seconds left!"

Ojohna stepped in and said, "I know what we need to do. When we were coming this way we passed a big ball of fire."

"The sun?" Chaos asked.

"Yeah." Ojohna said. "I'm one of the fastest people from the team. I'll do it. Just make sure you tell everybody that I said I'm sorry, that I won't be coming back. And please protect our planet."

Ojohna picked up the box and flew off. In just seconds he was already out of the Earth's atmosphere and flying through space. He got closer and closer to the sun and his skin began to boil, his flesh was burning. There was a timer countdown on the side of the box. There were ten seconds remaining as he was flying towards the sun.

Just as Ojohna was fifty feet away from the surface of the sun, he threw the box into the sun and it was instantly destroyed on contact. Ojohna was trying to fly away from the sun, but the heat was too much and he burned to death.

Meanwhile back on Earth, Chaos said to the others, "He did it… The time has elapsed and nothing happened. But where is he at? He should have made it back by now."

Ojohna's partner closed his eyes and said, "He's not coming back. He probably couldn't survive the heat from the sun. Ojohna was my mentor, I looked up to him. He's a true hero, gave his life to save people from another planet."

All around the world, with all of the boxes destroyed the women were no longer under the control of

Crystal Jones. As things were starting to return to normal and the transmitting curse had been broken, people were starting to come together.

As the fight continued on between Crystal and Darkside, he had her in a rear choke-hold. "You've lost. Everything is returning back to normal! Your plans for genocide are cancelled."

Crystal started to laugh. She threw an elbow to the side of Darkside's ribs repeatedly but he refused to let her go as he stood behind her with the chokehold locked in. She was unable to free herself. She then kicked backwards, hitting Darkside right between the legs. The hold was broken. Crystal was released. She reached into the pocket of her pants and pulled out a bracelet, then snapped it on Darkside's left wrist. The bracelet began to glow. In pain, he tried to rip the bracelet off but wasn't able to.

Crystal suddenly punched Darkside right between the eyes and knocked him down. Darkside quickly stood back up and threw punches, left and rights, at Crystal but she blocked every one. Darkside was in shock that he couldn't land a single hit.

She then threw a left punch to his gut. She then grabbed his arm and threw him across the street into a building. As he hit the building, the wall broke and Darkside was thrown straight through. He slowly started to stand out of the rubble, and Crystal laughed once more.

"It seems the tables have turned!" Crystal proclaimed. "That bracelet that I attached to your wrist is weakening you. I have done my research. I know that Michael Smith is not from here, I know he has powers and I knew there would be others just like him. That bracelet will cut the strength of anyone it's attached to down to half!"

Chaos and the others all flew down. Darkside yelled out, "She disabled half of my power!"

Chaos said, "That's not gonna be a problem. We're all gonna take her out!"

Crystal laughed. "The only person that can beat me here is Darkside and he lost half of his abilities. The rest of you are just jokes."

CHAPTER 15:

CRYSTAL VS. EVERYONE

As there was a moment of silence, Crystal yelled out, "So are you guys going to continue to fight one-by-one or do you all want to die at the same time?"

Chaos then took off running at Crystal. He came swinging with a left hook that she ducked under, and then she turned around with a right elbow, hitting him in the ribs. Messiah and Trinity flew towards the two of them, but Crystal jumped out of the way. She did a backflip, landed right in front of Darkside, turned around, and elbowed him in the face.

Crystal grabbed Darkside, lifted him above her head and threw him at the group, knocking them all down. She began to walk towards all of them. She walked over, picked up Darkside and threw him across the street again. He fell into a fire hydrant and broke it. Water began shooting from the ground.

Chaos, Trinity, and Messiah all started swinging, throwing punches and kicks at Crystal. She was blocking and dodging all of their hits. Ojohna's partner flew in to attack her. Crystal saw him and threw a left hook, hitting him in the face and knocking him to the floor. The whole group ran and jumped on top of her to hold her down, but she powered out and knocked everyone off of her.

As all of this was happening, there was a man walking the streets near where the battle was taking place. The man appeared to be badly injured. As Crystal stood there laughing, Darkside got back up. He walked towards Crystal. "So you're back for more? You know as long as that bracelet is on your wrist you can't beat me. And you can't pull it off because if you try to pull it off, it'll weaken you further to prevent you from pulling it off."

As Darkside walked up to her, he was standing face-to-face. He threw a right punch at her. She knocked his hand away. She then punched him right in the gut and dropped him down to one knee. As Darkside and the others got back up Messiah said, "How are we gonna beat her? She's too strong and she's crippled Darkside's abilities!"

"I don't know but we'll find a way." Chaos replied.

As Darkside was down on one knee in pain, Crystal grabbed him, picked him up above her head once again and threw him. After Darkside was tossed through the air, he hit the ground two blocks away. She then ran over, picked him up by the leg, jumped into the air and flew off.

She slammed him, letting go and knocking him down to the ground. Chaos and the others came in to attack Crystal. Crystal side-stepped him, throwing a right hook to Chaos, knocking him down to the ground. Then she followed up with a roundhouse kick that knocked Trinity to the ground.

She then grabbed Ojohna's partner throwing him to the side, then went after Messiah, tackling him to the ground. Crystal descended from the air, grabbed Darkside by the ankle and began dragging him while walking down the street. Holding onto his left ankle, she flung him, smacking him into a parked car but she held on to his leg and continued dragging him, then slammed him into another parked car, and continued dragging him. Chaos came rushing out of nowhere to attack Crystal from behind. Using her free hand, she stopped him by grabbing him by the neck and slamming him to the ground.

Crystal continued to walk. Chaos got back up and flew in for another attack but she side-stepped and threw Darkside into him, knocking them both down. Crystal stood there laughing.

As she stood there enjoying the moment, the man who was walking who was badly damaged walked up to the Seattle Space Needle. He stopped right outside the building to catch his breath. As this was going on, back at the White House the President of the United States was at a meeting. He was with the Secretary of Defense and the Vice President. The President picked up a phone and made a call. He said, "I want you to send a team in to Seattle where this is taking place. We need to stop this. Take down the enemy by any means necessary.

In moments there were three helicopters heading over to where Crystal and the others were at. Two military tanks rolled up just outside of the Seattle Space Needle. The ramp door dropped from both trucks and a team of nine men came out of each truck. They set up a perimeter and pointed their weapons at Crystal. A humvee pulled up as well. Three men got out of the humvee. Crystal started laughing. She said, "So now the military wants to get involved with my business?" Crystal walked over and grabbed Chaos by the ankle and flung him right towards one of the helicopters in the sky. Upon impact the helicopter went down in an explosion and the helicopter and Chaos both fell out of the sky crashing to the ground.

A captain from the group of three that had gotten out of the humvee yelled, "Open fire!" All of the troops began shooting directly at Crystal. The bullets were bouncing off of her. She laughed, as their attack was futile. A fighter jet was approaching and the pilot had his sights locked on Crystal. He pressed the button, unleashing a missile.

Crystal jumped into the air towards the missile, grabbed it, and threw it right back at the pilot who had shot it. The aircraft exploded and fell toward the ground. The captain was in charge of the team yelled, "Fall back! Fall back!"

The troops began to retreat while Crystal laughed maniacally. Crystal then walked over, grabbed Darkside by the neck with her left hand. She stood him up and holding onto him, she flew up into the air. She flew to the top of the Space Needle and hooked the back of his shirt to the tip of the point at the very top of the structure. As Darkside was hanging there seemingly lifeless, Crystal threw a left punch to his stomach and a right punch to his face.

While he still hung there not moving an inch, she took off and returned to the ground. Trinity, Messiah, and Ojohna's partner came running up. Crystal ran towards the three of them. She hit Messiah head-on, knocking him to the ground, then grabbed Ojohna's partner and smacked him right into Trinity, knocking him down. Crystal stood up and grabbed Messiah's ankle with one hand and Trinity's ankle with another hand. She flung Trinity in one direction and Messiah through another, knocking them through buildings.

She then walked over to Ojohna's partner as he laid on the ground trying to crawl away.

"You're not going anywhere." Crystal told Ojohna's partner. She walked over and stomped on his back, grinding her heel into his back. He yelled out in pain as she said to him, "You thought it was over. You thought you had me beat! You were all under the assumption that you won, but how do you like it? Now you're gonna fall and it's only a matter of time before I rebuild the boxes and continue where I left off."

In severe pain, he cried out to Crystal, "You're crazy, that's what you are! You're just straight crazy. I don't know why you are, but you're just a worthless villain who thinks that everybody owes them something."

"Worthless, you say?" Crystal asked. "I'm not worthless." She then took her foot off of his back and turned him over. As he laid there in pain barely able to move, she walked over and put her foot on his neck. She said out to him, "I hope your little speech was worth it. Interfering with my plan just cost you your life." She continued to press down on his neck until it snapped. He stopped moving and blood ran from his mouth as he lay there, lifeless.

She then began walking back over to where Darkside and Chaos were. Chaos was face-down on the ground, not moving an inch. Darkside continued to hang lifelessly on top of the Space Needle. As it seemed all hope was lost and death was in the air from the carnage that was all around, Crystal flew up to the top of the Space Needle and pulled Darkside off the tip of the structure. She picked him up and threw him down to the ground right by where

Chaos was laying. As the two brothers lay there not moving an inch. With the two brothers laying there, it seemed all hope was lost. Messiah came rushing straight through and tried to attack Crystal but he was no match. She grabbed him and threw him down on the ground by Darkside and Chaos.

Crystal walked over to the three of them and said, "Look at the three pieces of trash that need to be thrown away. I snapped the neck of the other one, now I will do the same with you three. Who wants to die first?"

Darkside started to move. His face was badly bruised and his right eye was bloody and bruised shut. He was trying to make an effort to stand up but was having trouble. Crystal just laughed. She said out to him, "You're the only one that could have beat me, but you missed your chance."

Trinity yelled out, "Yo bitch! You crazy nut job!" Crystal looked over and saw an injured Trinity walking slowly towards her.

Crystal yelled out to her, "You want another shot? Why don't you just go somewhere and die, you traitor?" Trinity kept approaching Crystal. Crystal yelled out, "Why don't you come lay down next to the rest of the trash and accept your fate?"

Trinity then took off running as fast as she could up to Crystal, then swung and threw punches but to no avail. Crystal was just too fast and strong for her. Crystal then slapped Trinity, knocking her down to the ground next to the others. Crystal laughed, saying, "It looks like the tank is on empty! You can't even land a punch anymore! Let it be known that the fall of mankind started today. And how these fools tried to oppose me. But what I say is law. Don't worry, I won't kill all of the men. They will make good slaves as they serve, and trust me. All of you will be missed by all of the men who will bow down after you're gone."

Crystal flew to the top of the Space Needle just underneath the bottom of the dome and started pulling, causing it to break. As she ripped it off the body of the structure, she held it over her head and yelled, "Now all of you can DIE!!!" She threw the structure down to them.

As the top of the Space Needle came down about to crash on Darkside and all of the others, Darkside rolled over on top of the three of them. The top of the Space Needle smashed into them. Crystal was laughing and descended back to the ground. She walked over to the broken structure of the building and yelled out, "Victory is mine!"

CHAPTER 16:

FORGIVENESS

As Crystal laughed sadistically, she felt that she had won. She slowly started to walk away. As it seemed that all hope was lost, the top of the Space Needle began to move. Crystal instantly stopped and turned around. The Space Needle stopped moving. She started to walk back to the wreckage. Standing back where the broken structure was, she was looking around but there was no movement at all.

She slowly turned around and started to walk off again and as she was walking away, the structure started to lift off the ground. She stopped and turned around and was in shock. Suddenly the structure was thrown fifty feet back. Crystal could not believe her eyes. Standing there was Darkside!

She yelled out to him, "How is this possible? All of you were crushed underneath that building! There's no way you could have survived!"

He said nothing as he stood there staring at her. As the others laid on the ground looking up at Darkside, Chaos asked his brother, "Are you gonna hold back this time?"

Darkside did not say a word. He slowly started walking towards Crystal. Crystal started slowly walking towards him. As the two met face-to-face staring in each other's eyes, there was a silence still in the air. With a look of rage on her face, she swung with a right hook at Darkside but he caught her fist.

She tried to swing with her other hand but he knocked it away. In great shock, Crystal took a step back. She yelled out, "You're supposed to be dead!"

Darkside then kicked Crystal right in the center of her chest, knocking her fifty feet back. As she hit the ground and was standing up, Darkside was already right by her side. She couldn't believe it as she was crawling backwards on the ground and muttered the words, "How could this be? There's no way. You should be dead. All of you should be dead. There's no way. You couldn't even stand up!"

Darkside yelled at her. "Stand up!" Crystal slowly stood up and had a look of horror on her face. She was as pale as if she had seen a ghost. Frozen in fear as she stood there, Darkside asked her in a stern voice, "Are you sorry for what you've done?"

Crystal was so shocked in fear that she didn't say a word. He asked her again, but she said nothing. Now with anger in his voice he asked her again, "Are you sorry for what you've done? For all the lives you've ended today? For all the pain you caused? Are you sorry?"

Crystal put her head down and said very quietly, "I'm not sorry. I used to be sorry, but I'm not sorry anymore." She rose up her head with anger in her voice now and said, "Look what has happened to me, all because of men. They're the reason the world is such a horrible place, all because of them. They did this. Not me."

Crystal suddenly tried to punch with a right fist but he caught it and put her in a hammerlock. As he stood behind her, he said to her, "You are blind. You're taking your anger, your emotions, your rage, out on innocent people. You've been wronged in the past many times, but what you're doing is uncalled for like I said before.

And since you have no sympathy or sorrow for all the lives you've taken and damage you've caused, it's time for you to go."

As he held her arm behind her back in the lock, the same man who appeared to be badly injured and beaten was walking towards where Darkside and Crystal were. Chaos, Trinity and Messiah were watching what was going on when the man suddenly walked up to them. The man yelled out, "Where's Crystal? Where is she at?"

Trinity turned and looked at the man and said, "You mean that crazy nut job that tried to kill every man on the planet and cause genocide and shape the world in her sick twisted mind?"

The man said to Trinity, "No, you're wrong. She's just hurt." The man continued to walk as he left the group.

As the man made his way towards Darkside and Crystal, Darkside let Crystal go. Crystal turned around and elbowed Darkside right in the face, but he just stood there. She turned around and punched him in the face, and in the throat, in the side of his ribs but he merely stood there not moving an inch. Crystal then jumped high into the sky.

As she stopped what appeared to be a hundred feet in the air, she looked and Darkside was standing right there. She was shocked, and couldn't believe it.

Crystal made one more attack at Darkside, throwing a straight punch right for him but he caught her arm and was clutching her right wrist.

Crystal yelled out, "How can this be? That bracelet should have drained half of your power! There's no way you could be this strong!"

With a look of disgust on his face, he said to her, "You're taking your unhappiness out on everyone. I can't allow you to do that. You may have altered your body and made yourself stronger than a normal human but no matter what you put in your body you're still human."

As he held her right wrist from the punch that she tried to hit him with, Darkside used his left hand and snapped the bone right beneath her wrist. Tears ran down Crystal's face as she cried out in excruciating pain. Darkside, still holding on to her arm, threw her straight down to the ground. As Crystal's body hit the ground and the pavement cracked with her indentation in the concrete, Darkside turned and looked at her.

Tears were running down Crystal's face as she laid there on the ground, knowing that she was about to meet her demise and it was all over. Darkside yelled out, "Crystal Jones! It's time for you to pay for all that you have done!"

As Crystal's eyes were open wide and tears continued to run down her eyes, Darkside took his right hand and put it above his left shoulder. The man who had walked up gravely injured suddenly ran as fast as he could and ran to Crystal's side and sat her up, wrapping his arms around her. Darkside was shocked by this gesture and yelled out, "What are you doing? Get out of the way!"

The man looked up at Darkside and said, "No!"

With a look of shock on her face, Crystal said to the man, "Kenneth! What are you doing?"

He replied to her, "I love you. I've always loved you. And I just wanted you to know that I'm sorry for all the bad things men have done to you over the years."

She looked at him with disbelief and asked, "What are you talking about?"

Kenneth said, "I've been working for you for the past four years as your assistant. I've known you for eight years. Ever since you were in high school I had seen all of the terrible things that happened to you, from your night at prom, your parents breaking up, what happened at college, even what happened with Arthur. I've always loved you. I was always there to comfort you and I put out little hints that someday you would see me as more than a friend, but the day never came. You were always in love with somebody else and never me.

I've been carrying this torch for you for over eight years and even though seeing what you've done today I still love you. I've always wanted to be with you, Crystal. And if this is the only chance I have, right before you die, I want to be right there with you."

Crystal had a look of shock and was speechless. Trinity and the others watched from the sideline and Trinity said, "I can't believe that guy is in love with that crazy nut job! He must be as messed up as she is."

Crystal then said out to Kenneth, "You would really sit here and die with me?"

"Yes. Yes I would." Kenneth told her.

As Crystal looked into his eyes, "All these years I've been searching for the right one and he was in front of my face the whole time. I feel so stupid. I wish I could undo all of the terrible things I've done, all of the lives I've taken. You shouldn't sit here and die with me, I brought this on myself."

Kenneth didn't say a word. He just held onto Crystal, clutching her tightly. He put his head on her shoulder and she continued to cry. Suddenly Darkside descended from the sky. He walked over to Crystal and Kenneth. As Darkside stood next to the two sitting on the ground, he put his hand out to Crystal. She looked up at him in shock and said, "You're not gonna kill me for all of the horrible things I've done?"

He replied to her, "No. I knew there was something special about you and there was good inside you. The only problem was you've been blind and didn't see it anymore.

Looks like you finally came out of the dark and can see again.

Crystal smiled and took Darkside's hand and stood up. Darkside said to her. "This is your second chance. Don't waste it. And from here on forth, you have to make amends for all that you've done."

Crystal replied with tears in her eyes, "I will."

Crystal then gave Darkside a hug and said, "Thank you for sparing Crystal's life…"

Chaos, Trinity and Messiah all came running up to the three of them. Chaos said, "Are you crazy brother? Are you just going to let her walk? Didn't you see all the damage that she's done? You're going to let her walk away from all of this?"

Trinity cut in and said, "Chaos is right. You've seen all of the lives she's destroyed. She tried to bring genocide and you're just gonna let her walk away?"

Darkside then turned to them and said, "Yes. She's learned her lesson and found the good that's in her once again."

Chaos then said, "But brother what happens if she goes crazy and decides to kill us all? We should take advantage of this opportunity to take her down."

"That won't be necessary." Darkside said. "If she ever does try anything, I'll take her out without any mercy. But I think she deserves a second chance."

With a look of shock on her face, Trinity said, "I'm starting to think you're as crazy as she is, Darkside."

Darkside then said, "Oh yeah. You're right. I forgot to take this stupid bracelet off!" He then took his right hand and broke the bracelet off of his wrist and dropped it to the ground. "Remember last time we were in that fight against Ramis and his brother and were about to die and I borrowed your power to beat them? I kind of did the exact same thing this time. I could have taken the bracelet off after that, but I forgot. "

Chaos just shook his head in disbelief. Darkside turned and looked at Crystal and Kenneth. He said to Crystal, "Now you've seen what it's like to be a villain. How about you come back on the good side?"

Crystal replied, "Yes. Yes I will."

Crystal and Darkside both shook hands. Finally the fight was over. Crystal Jones had been defeated and she had seen the error of her ways. Things could finally return back to normal. As the city of Seattle was slowly repairing itself from all the damage, Darkside, Chaos and Trinity were now on their way back home to their home planet to help in the fight for the war that was about to break out.

As Darkside and the others continued making their way back to the planet Ying Yang, Crystal Jones was in a press conference. As she stood in front of the cameras and the audience, she said, "My apologies to everyone. I know what I've done is wrong. All my life I've wanted to help people but instead I've done the opposite.

I thank Darkside and his friends for giving me a second chance and opening my eyes. Shamefully I have grown blind but I can see again and I thank them for that. From this day forward I will spend the rest of my life helping and protecting people. And I thank the love of my life,

Kenneth, for helping me and pushing me in the right direction."

As Crystal walked off the stage, Messiah walked off the stage and approached the microphone. A man in the audience yelled out, "Let's go Michael Smith! Yeah!"

While Messiah spoke to the crowd with all the viewers watching he said, "I know a lot of you are feeling impartial and some of you don't like the decision that we let her live, but she has seen the error of her ways.

And all of you can rest assured that if anything goes wrong with Crystal or anything else. I, my sister, Darkside and Chaos will all be here to take care of everything. We can't thank you enough for letting us live here on earth."

As the press conference continued on and Messiah continued to answer questions, Darkside, Chaos and Trinity were almost home to the planet Ying Yang. There was five war ships that was also heading right for the planet Ying Yang.

CHAPTER 17:

WAR ON YING YANG

I can't believe what is going on, it's just nonstop Trinity said. I know it crazy Chaos replied to her. All of the events that to place on earth with my brother have been cloned, to Crystal trying to take over the world. "It just seem like there is no break to rest" Trinity replied. Darkside then spoke out, "Times are hard right now. I also feel that it's just getting started." What do mean Trinity asked?

Think about it, we picked up April's sister from the airport. She found a box that got broken, and the 7 pieces all got up and flew away. The whole problem with Stan Jones and his sister may have been stopped, but I have a feeling that it's about to get even more crazy. Darkside said.

"I think your right Darkside" Trinity said. I just hope that when we all return back to earth, my brother is still alive and that nut job Crystal didn't take over the world. Don't worry Darkside replied, "I'm sure earth and your brother will be fine. I saw the good in Crystal." Let's hope it is there and will stay, she replied.

As the three of them continued on route back to Ying Yang, the five war ships had already made their way to the planet. The alarms around the South Division area of the planet were all going off. Major Barrel, the new Division leader that had taken over after Chaos left with his brother to earth. Was waiting at the landing zone area waiting for Chaos and the others to arrive. As the five war ships had finally arrived, soldier of the Ying Yang military were in places. The ships parked all in straight line, side by side.

The doors began to open, and a ramp came unfolding from all of the ships. The two ships on the end of left and right, had hundreds of troops come marching out. This army didn't have any type of gun, but instead had swords. As the soldiers of the Ying Yang military were posted up in position, a figure was now standing in the door way of the center ship. Back at the landing zone, Darkside and the other had finally arrived.

Major Barrel quickly walked to the ship to meet them. As everyone got out of the ship, Barrel had a look of confusion on his and asked. "Where is Ojohna and Redox?"

Chaos replied, "They didn't make it" What do you mean Barrel asked. "They didn't make it back with us." That's right Darkside said, "We was in the middle of a battle when they came to earth. If it wasn't for them, things could have went a lot worse. They lost their lives in battle with us."

I can't believe it, Barrel said. Ojohna is one of the strongest fighters I know. It is hard to believe Darkside said, but he helped save millions of lives before he was taken out. Barrel put his head down. So what is going on? Darkside asked.

Something horrible Barrel said. "We had got a transmission a few days about a pending attack on our planet." What do you mean Darkside asked.

Yes, Barrel replied. The messaged stated that a war was coming, and that the people of Ying Yang would pay. That's crazy Chaos said. "I can't believe someone wants to attack our home. After all we do so much good to help others."

I know, Barrel said. "This is why I had sent Ojohna and Redox to come bring you back to help fight with us." It would be an honor to help in the battle to keep our home safe. Chaos said. My brother and Trinity are here to help as well. Thank you Barrel replied, "Your father would be proud of the both of you." Is the military in place for the attack? Chaos asked. Yes they are Barrel replied. "Well, we should get going and meet up with everyone else." Chaos said.

Barrel nodded his head, and the four of them took off running to south division area. As they were on the way, the strange figure that was standing in the door way of the center ship started walking. As this unknown figure walked down the ramp, then between all of the troops. One of the division judges stepped forward from a group of Ying Yang soldiers. The unknown figure walked in front of all the troops to meet face to face with the division judge. The unknown man stood at 9 feet tall, and had a body that was a thick as a tree trunk. With dark grey skin, and had what looked to be a dark grey metallic body armor on. The monster had bright blue eyes, and short black spikes that stuck out of the top of his head.

"Who are you and what is the reason you have come to our planet?" The judge asked. The monster replied, "I am Frost! Your planet has been picked to be taken over. All of your people can surrender, and become slaves."

The judge replied, "Slaves? You want us to all surrender, and be slaves? We will not be your slaves!"

Have it your way Frost said. "We will kill you all and take the planet from you then!"

Finally Major Barrel also with Darkside and the others had arrived to scene. Barrel, Darkside, Chaos, and Trinity all stood right behind the judge. The evil monster looked at all of them and said. "Just who are these who have decided to come forward?"

Barrel spoke out, "I am Major Barrel, the leader of the South Division for Ying Yang."

So you're the leader of this planet and all of the waste of life that I see before myself? Barrel then said, "Waste of life?" That's right Frost said. "A waste of life. You will die today, and your people will die along with you!"

That's not gonna happen Barrel said. "Is that so" Frost replied. "Look around Barrel, my soldiers don't wear armor, because they don't need it. They don't have guns to fire, because they don't need it. They don't need to shoot from a distance, because they don't need to."

It doesn't matter what the need or don't need. Barrel said. "We will stop them, and you! Leave now before it is too late!"

Too late? Ha ha ha…. Frost laughed. My soldiers will destroy you all! "No one of this planet will live!"

Well, if it is a fight to the death you want. Then that's what you will get! Barrel said. "Just don't be shocked when you lose and the death of all your troops will be on your hands. Then when your death has come."

You're very hopeful Frost laughed. There is no way that you will live, let alone defeat us! "You all will DIE TODAY!" Your planet has been picked to be the new area of operations. So all of this junk, and I mean waste of space. The very waste of life that is on this planet needs to be removed! "So Major Barrel, declare war on Ying Yang!"

All of the Ying Yang soldier rushed at all of the troops from the army of Frost. Shots were fired, and swords flying left and right. Both sides was starting to take a losses. Barrel rush right for Frost, as the two of them clashed exchanging punches. Darkside, Chaos and Trinity was moving all around attacking the evil troops from Frost's army.

As Frost and Barrel continued to exchange hits, a loud roar came from the center spaceship that Frost had walked out from. Chaos looked over to see what was going on. A monster that stood at about 12 feet tall, that had body as thick as an oak tree walked out. The monster had red skin, and black small spikes that was coming out of it back. With pure whites eyes, and teeth like a piranha.

"What in the world is that thing?" Chaos yelled out.

As Frost continued to exchange hits with Barrel, he looked over at the monster with red skin and asked. "What is that thing?" Frost just laughed. The red skinned monster let out a roar so loud it felt like it could shake the heavens. Frost laughed as he continued fight with Barrel, as Darkside, Chaos and Trinity continued to take down the troops of Frost's army.

Frost now started blocking more and more of Barrel's attacks. "Looks like you are not as skilled as you think you are" he said to Barrel. Well, don't worry you won't have to live long in your time of pain. "COME KILL THEM ALL MY BEAST" Frost yelled out.

The red skinned monster now started walking down the ramp of the ship to join the battle. Three soldiers of the Ying Yang military ran up to monster shooting it with their weapons, but it had no effect on him. The monster then his right hand covered one of the soldiers by the face and crushed his head.

The soldier fell to the ground dead. The red monster then knocked the other two back about ten feet with a single swipe. Just as it seem the Ying Yang military was gaining the upper hand in the fight, they how to face this monster of Frost. Chaos called out to his brother and Trinity "we are gonna have to take that thing down!" Trinity replied, your right.

As Frost and Barrel continued fighting, Barrel wasn't landing any hits at all on Frost. "Time for you to meet your maker" Frost laughed. Frost ducked and moved side to side as Barrel continued to hit him. Frost spoke out, "enough of this game! Time for you to die." Frost the put his hand around Barrel's neck and slammed him into the ground. Before Barrel could move, Frost stomped his right foot on his chest. Barrel cried out in pain, as Frost pressed his foot into his body.

Frost then bent over and grabbed Barrel's left arm, and stared to pulling at it. "Look Barrel!" Frost yelled at him. Do you see how your soldiers are dying left and right at the hands of my monster? LOOK AT ALL THE BODIES!!! As Barrel was in pain and couldn't defend himself, Frost then smiled looking down at him and ripped his left arm from Barrel's body.

Frost laughed out loud as Barrel cried out in pain. He then dropped his arm right next to him. Frost took his foot off of him, and sat him up. As Barrel was losing blood fast. Frost grabbed him by the back of his head, "look at all of your soldiers die!" The monster was killing them no problem. The fight had changed, and the Ying Yang military was now losing the battle. Darkside yelled out, Chaos, Trinity, we need to stop that monster! Trinity and Chaos both jumped in front of the red monster. The monster let out a loud roar. Chaos and Trinity looked at each then back at the monster. "Darkside, we could use your help right about now" Trinity yelled out.

Frost laughed, so is this your back up plan Barrel? You think these fools are gonna stop the death of your planet today? Barrel replied, as he continued to bleed, Chaos was the Major here before, and was undefeated. Chaos and his brother will stop your monster and you. "We will see about that" Frost said. As Chaos and Trinity both were standing in front of the monster, it reached out to grab Chaos, but he jumped to side. The monster roared, and then tried to reach out at him again.

Chaos jumped into the air, but this time, red monster grabbed him his left leg. Trinity rushed right for the monster to help Chaos, but she as well stopped. The monster had grabbed her by her waist. It roared, as it looked at Chaos and Trinity holding them both. "Ha ha ha, do you see this Barrel?" Frost laughed. The monster lifted his arms in the air as he held Chaos and Trinity. Just before he could smashed them into the ground, Darkside flying at the red monster and kneed it right between the eyes knocking him down.

As the monster fell over, it made him release Chaos and Trinity from the attack by Darkside.

What?! Frost yelled out. How could he knock him down that easy? Barrel spoke out in words or joy, "that is the brother of Chaos, I didn't know he was that strong. Looks like your monster has met his match." Shut up, Frost replied. He just got a luck hit. That guy is gonna die with the rest of your sorry excuse for an army.

As Darkside stood with his brother and Trinity, the monster got back up and roared at the three of them. Darkside looked over at his brother and said. "Go help Barrel and take down Frost. I will take care of this monster." Chaos replied, what are you crazy? We need to fight this beast together! No Darkside said, I will handle this. You and Trinity help Barrel and stop Frost. Chaos and Trinity both walked away, and Darkside now stood in front of the red monster alone. The monster roared and reached out that grab Darkside, but he jump into the air. The monster then jump up to grab him again, but he move quickly to the left avoiding the monster once again.

As Darkside was standing in the air, monster land back on the ground. It turned it's backside to Darkside, and suddenly the black spikes that were on the monster's back came flying out. As the spikes were flying fast right for Darkside, he moved left and right, up and down. Darkside was able to avoid every single spike without getting hit at all.

Darkside then jumped down and landed on the ground. As he continued the fight with the red beast, Chaos and Trinity both stood in front of Frost. "Step away from Major Barrel" Chaos yelled out. Frost stood there laughing at them. So, the old Major that ran away and his joke of side kick is gonna stop me? Do you not see what I did to this fool right here? Trinity replied, who are you calling a sidekick?!

"Well, since you think you are so powerful, why don't you come stop me sidekick" Frost said laughing.

Trinity rushed at him, but as she came flying in with a right hook. Frost stopped her attack as he grabbed her arm before she could strike him. Frost laughed at her, "come on sidekick, what's wrong? Go run along little one and let the warriors handle business." Said with a smile on his face.

Chaos flew right for Frost to help Trinity, but before he could attack Frost. Two laser beams came from he's eyes and hit Chaos as he was about to hit Frost. Chaos was stopped in midair and dropped right to the ground. Chaos had a look of shock on his face, and it seemed he was paralyzed. "Looks like the B Team has failed" frost laughed.

As Chaos and Trinity seemed to be at the mercy of Frost, Darkside was still fight with the red monster. Still unable to hit Darkside, as he moved quickly using his speed to avoid attacks from the monster. Darkside smiled, and the red skinned monster. The monster took off running right for him, and he took off running at the red monster as well. Darkside jumped forward spearing him right in the gut. The monster dropped to the ground.

Darkside then stood up on the chest of his red foe and lifted up his right hand then drove it down, cutting into the body of the monster. The monster yelled out in pain, and then Darkside let off his signature move and with his right hand in the body of the beast. A blast let out and the monster exploded.

As the dust settled, and smoke cleared. Darkside was there on one knee with his hand to the ground. He then stood up, and turned around looking at Frost. He saw his brother on the ground, and Trinity being locked under the grip of Frost by her arm.

CHAPTER 18:

DARKSIDE VS. FROST

As Darkside looked over and saw what was going on, he took out running right for Frost.

"Looks like the two you are no match for me" Frost said,

"We will stop you" Trinity replied.

Frost just smiled as Chaos was still unable to move, and he had a hold on Trinity as she wasn't able to free herself from his hold. Darkside rushed to the scene, and walked over to his brother on the ground. How do you like? Frost asked. Your brother the old Major and Barrel, the new one both helpless to stop me.

You have lost your mind, Darkside replied. "You come to my home and attack my friends, family, and my people. And for what?!"

Don't get all mighty with me you worthless worm! Frost replied.

This is your chance to pack up and leave before I break you in half, Darkside said.

So the mighty brother of the old washed up Major is gonna stop me. It's clear you have no idea who you are talking to! Frost yelled.

All I know is that the one responsible for all that has happened here is you. Darkside replied.

Well, these three have tried to stop me and look where they are at. I don't have a no problem killing you to! I see that you are not scared, but that's all about to change. You should run before I rip you in half. Frost said.

"I don't bend, I don't break, and I don't back down!" Darkside yelled out. "Well, let us fight" Frost replied. Frost stilling holding Trinity by the arm, slammed her into the ground. Darkside came rushing at Frost, the two of them met head on exchanging punches and kicks. Not bad, Frost said. You have some skill that's for sure. Now the question is can you keep it up?

Darkside replied, Oh, I'm just getting started Frost.

Frost and Darkside continued to exchange hit after hit. Looked as the two were on the same level. Frost jumped back away from Darkside, but leaped at him. Darkside jumped out of the way, and up into the air.

Frost quickly flew after him. "Where do you think you're going?" Frost yelled out. Darkside stopped in midair, and then quickly drove down right for him. Darkside tackled him, and the two hit the ground.

As Darkside was mounted on top of him, he hit Frost with and right punches to the face. After taking a series of hits the face. Frost seemed to be out cold from the hits. Darkside slowly got up and stood next to him, "Get up!" Darkside said. I know you're not done, and you can hear me. Frost began to laugh, and his eyes opened up. As he stood up, he smiled right at Darkside. "Not bad, you have some power behind your punches. In fact, you have moves like a little pest that I was gonna kill some time ago." Frost said to him. What are you talking about? Darkside asked.

You're the second one to tell me that. Moves like who? Who is this girl? Darkside asked. Frost had a moment of confusion on his face. He was puzzled by the fact that Darkside didn't know to what he was talking about.

Nevertheless Frost said." It doesn't matter who you fight like, you will still die. I have destroyed lives, taken over planets, and took top class warriors and broke them before their demise. You are no different from any of the others I have crushed!"

Darkside replied to him, "You are strong, and have destroyed many lives I'm sure of it. But you will not win here today. You are just a bully and a heartless monster! You find joy in others pain, and you for your own gain. The nightmare that you have disturbed so many with, ends right here!"

I am gonna enjoy killing you, Frost said. I will cut your skin off your worthless body and use it a floor mat in my spaceship.

Darkside rushed at Frost and punched him right in the mouth. As Frost was starting to fall backwards, Darkside hit with a left punch to the gut. As Frost now bent forward form the second hit, Darkside followed up with a series of hits all over the body and face of Frost. Frost wasn't able to block any of the hits as his face was starting to bleed. The orange blood was starting to run down his face. Darkside stopped for a moment, but then jumped up and hit him with an elbow to his face. Frost hit the ground hard, and continued to bleed.

Darkside walked over to him, but Frost wasn't done just yet. He grabbed Darkside the right leg and with great strength, he pulled. Darkside fell to the ground. Frost stood up quickly and kicked him right in his side. Frost was in rage, and bent down and pick up Darkside with both hands around his neck. "You worthless bug! How dare you do this to me?" Frost held him by the neck in the air.

Darkside's feet were no longer touching the ground. "After I kill you, I will kick your brother, your side kick, and Barrel!" Frost let go of Darkside, as his feet landed on the ground. Frost kicked him right in the chest with a powerful right kick. The hit knocked Darkside 100 feet back and into a tank. Darkside hit the military tank and fell to the ground face first. Frost ran over to Darkside's body.

As he laid on the ground face down, not moving at all. Frost started to laugh, "This is the might hero that was gonna save everyone and stop me? What a joke."

Trinity and Chaos wasn't able to help Darkside. The troops of Frost had the soldiers of the Ying Yang military that was still alive, down on the ground all tied up by a dark blue rope. Frost then stomped on Darkside's Head. The impact of the stomp, pushed Darkside whole head into the ground. Frost continued stomping on his body all the way down until Darkside whole body was stomped into the ground and couldn't be seen.

"Now that I have got rid of the trash, it's time to take out the family and friends." Frost laughed with a sinister look on his face. Chaos was still paralyzed for the attack, and Trinity was still out cold from being slammed into the ground. Frost walked over to Trinity and put his foot on her face. He smiled and said, "I will put the side kick in the ground as well."

Frost lifted up his massive foot in the air, and just before he could bring it down to stomp Trinity's face in to the ground to kill her, Barrel shot a blast from his right hand. The energy ball hit Frost right in the face. Frost stopped and turned look right at Barrel. "So you want to die before her? No problem, I was gonna kill you last, but I can kill you now, since you can't seem to wait your turn!" Frost yelled at him.

Frost started walking to Barrel. With a scared look on his face, Barrel tried his best to stand up, but wasn't able to get off the ground. Frost walked over to him and kicked him right in the face knock him over. Frost stomped his left foot on the center of the body of Barrel. He bent over and grabbed the ankle of Barrel and started to pull.

As Frost stated to laugh, he ripped the right leg right off of Barrel. "Now you have one arm and leg missing. I think I should pull of the other two as well. What do you think Barrel?" Now with two limbs gone, the blood was just pouring out. Frost then started to press his foot into the body of Barrel. He yelled out in pain.

As it seemed that this was it for Barrel, and the foot of Frost started cut into his body. There was a massive explosion, and all of the Frost's troops fell to the ground. Frost turned around and stepped off of Barrel's body. As Frost was looking around trying to figure out what had just happed. The area was filled with smoke and dust. Frost continued look all over and started walking around, until he saw the figure of a man standing off to the side. Frost yelled, "What is going on?"

The figure in the smoke started to walk right for Frost. The smoke and dust started to clear, and Frost saw Darkside walking his way. Frost looked like he had seen a ghost, as he stood there frozen in fear. Darkside walked right up to Frost and had cold stare on his face. Frost then hit Darkside with a right punch to the face, but didn't do anything.

Darkside then hit Frost with a right hook to the left side of his body. To punch dug into him, and Frost started to bleed. Darkside pulled his fist for Frost's body. Frost was now holding his side and he was bleeding from where the punch was at.

Darkside hit Frost in the center of his body with a right and his fist went into his body. Darkside ripped out the spine of Frost. Frost fell to the ground and was losing blood fast. Darkside dropped his spine right on him. "You should have killed me when you had the chance, now I will finish you.

You come here to my home and take the lives of the people from Ying Yang. Time for you go!" Darkside pointed his right hand at Frost and dropped down to one knee. Darkside put his hand right in Frost body where the whole from his spine getting ripped out. Frost looked up at Darkside, for he knew his life was over. "DARKSIDE BLAST!" Darkside yelled out loud. Frost's body just exploded and he was gone.

Chaos was no longer paralyzed and stood up. Darkside walked over to Trinity and picked her up in his arms. Chaos walked over to Barrel and helped him. All of the troops of Frost where frozen in fear.

Their leader has been defeated. Chaos walked over to them and yelled at them to get on the ground. They quickly did what he said. As Barrel fell back over, Trinity started to wake up and her eyes opened up.

Darkside asked her if she was ok, and she smiled. As the area was destroyed from the battle that took place, it was now time to pick and rebuild. Darkside put Trinity down, and said. "I got a feeling that this is just the beginning."

CHAPTER 19:

RISE OF EVIL

Chaos and Trinity were on their way back to earth, but Darkside stayed on Ying Yang. As they were in route back to earth, Trinity was worried. "I hope that when we get back home, my brother is still alive and that nut job Crystal hasn't taken over the world." She said. Things will be okay Chaos replied.

I am just worried, I hope Darkside was right about letting her live. She did so much wrong and nearly killed half of the planet. Trinity spoke out in worry.

As they continued onward back to earth, Darkside was still on Ying Yang. He was at the recovery center with Barrel. As Barrel was in a recovery bed, Darkside was standing next to him. "Barrel, you knew my father, right?" Darkside asked. I did Barrel replied to him. Your father was a great warrior, truly one of a kind.

Darkside smiled as he was always very proud of his father. Darkside then asked Barrel, "Did you fight side by side with him? I remember the stories that he would tell my brother and I when we was just kids." Barrel smiled at Darkside and said, "Your father was the best! I met him back when I was a rookie. I had only been a part of the team for short time. Your father had been fighting for our planet and others for a while already. He was always willing to give it all he had and more, as long as it was for what was right." I wish would have got to fight by my father's side, Darkside replied.

I know Barrel said. "What makes you stay here on Ying Yang? Your brother and Trinity went back to earth." Barrel asked. Darkside looked at him and spoke with a look worry. "I stayed here, because I need to be here for now." What do you mean Barrel asked. "I know that a storm is coming" Darkside said.

Everything will be fine Barrel replied. From the moment that I met your father, I knew that he was hero. I know that your brother and you will be just as great as your father was.

Thank you Darkside replied. Meanwhile back on earth, things were starting to return to normal as it seemed. However, a storm had come to the lower half of the United States. It had been raining all of the cities in the state of Arizona, New Mexico, Texas, Louisiana and Mississippi. As this strange event was being covered all of the news, people all around the world talking about this unforeseen event of weather. There was a man that was being interviewed in Oklahoma City.

The report asked the man, "Do you fear that the strange down pour of rain will come to the state of Oklahoma?" The man replied to her, "I think the end is coming." Why do say that she asked? "For a while the weather hasn't been normal, there is a reason for all of this. I believe that the end is coming." The end? She asked, what do you mean the end? "There is so much chaos in the world today. It's time things to be rest, to be cleaned." So you are saying that end of the world is coming? She asked. "Yes! Are you not listening to what I am saying?!" The man then walked off.

The reporter then said to the camera, "Well I'm Jane Blackwell from Channel 18 News, here in Oklahoma City, Oklahoma."

As the news report continued talking to the camera, far away in Rome Italy. There four friends that all were on vacation. Two couples that were out having dinner at a restaurant. As the two couple sat at the table waiting for the food to arrive, all talking about how much they were enjoying the vacation in Rome. A man walked up to the table with a violin and started playing.

Then group all stopped talking as the man continued playing the violin. The room suddenly went dark, and there was a group of men and woman came to the table all holding lit candles. As the group of men and woman circled the four friends at the table, one the guys sitting at the table put his hand on his girlfriend's hand. "Ashley, I know that we have only been together for a year. I know in my heart that I love you and you are the reason I feel alive." She was just speechless as tears of joy ran down her face. "Ashley, you are my world. Just as these men and woman have lighted the path to this table, I want to light the path for you and always be there by your side till the day I die. Will you please give me the honor and make me the luckiest man in the world, and be my wife?" Ashley replied yes.

Tom then pulled a box out of his jacket pocket and opened it. He then took the ring out, and put it on Ashley's finger. The two of them kissed and everyone in the restaurant cheered and the light came back on. Everyone seemed to be happy for Tom and Ashley, but her friend seemed to be a bit unhappy.

Later after dinner, the four of them were back in the hotel room. Ashley was sitting on the looking at her ring. "I am so happy!" Ashley cried out. I can't believe I am getting married she spoke out in joy. Kim replied, with what looked to be a fake smile. "I'm so happy for you, you are just so lucky." Ashley looked up at her with a shocked look on her face. "Are you not happy for me and Tom?"

Kim replied, "You have everything, you got promoted at work. You come from a rich family, you have only been with Tom for a year, and now getting married. I have been with John for 5 years, and he has asked to marry me. We have been together since high school, and all this time he hasn't asked me to marry him. I bet he never will.

You just have everything Ashley! I wish I could have your life, just get to live in your shoes."

As Kim dropped to her knees and was crying,

She suddenly started screaming in pain. As she fell over on the floor holding her head with hands, a small sharp metal started coming out of her head. The metal was covered in blood. As soon as the small metal that covered in blood as out, the pain went away. Kim stood up quickly and was scared. There was no signs of a cut on her forehead where the metal had fell out of. As Kim bent over to pick of the small metal covered in blood. It lifted up from floor, and flew out of the window. The two girls looked at each other not saying a word.

Finally Chaos and Trinity had made it back to earth. They all were at April's place like always. "I'm glad you guys are back! Where is Darkside?" April asked. He stayed on Ying Yang Chaos replied. "Why would he do that?" She continued to ask. I don't know Chaos said. Messiah cut in, "I bet there is a reason why, Darkside has a plan for something."

I don't know what my brother is planning, or why he decided to stay there for a while, but I know he has a good reason for it. Chaos said.

Trinity then spoke out, "There is something coming, and it's big. Darkside had talked about a storm coming."

Everyone just looked at each other. As the weather continued in a strange way. Darkside back on Ying Yang dress as if he was ready for battle. He stood there outside, as he had a green tank top on, with his black pants and black boots. With black finger gloves, and cuffs with three foot chain on both of his wrists and ankles. He then started walking down to a building that looked to be made out of nothing but steel.

Meanwhile back on earth, April and her sister where getting ready to go out. April was all dressed up in a black dress and high heels. Her sister walked in dressed the same. Trinity made the comment to them, "You both are not twins, why are dressing alike?" April replied, "Some couples do it and sometimes brothers and sisters do it." Trinity looked at them confused. Chaos then said, "My brother and I never have dressed the same." April replied, "You both wear black pants all the time. If it wasn't for me, you would still being dressing the same." Chaos said, "We dress that way for battle." April laughed, "Chaos, you and brother both look better with some normal apparel. Even you to Trinity."

Trinity seemed to be in her own little world as she was just look to the side as mumbling. "He looks good no matter how he is dressed" April yelled out, "Hey, hey, Trinity, are you daydreaming about Darkside?" Trinity replied, "NO!" April just laughed, "Yes you are Trinity, I know you like Darkside, what's not to like? After all he has that nice tan skin, like Chaos. He isn't tall, but be he is hot!" Trinity started to turn red. Trinity, then turned her head and asked if they were ready to go out. As Trinity was trying to change the subject of her and Darkside.

As they all went out for a night on the town, Darkside was walking around in a dark room looked to have strange looking objects in the background. He was looking around all over the room, as there was strange noises in the room. The room must have been the size of a football field. As the Darkside continued walking around in the dark, and as Chaos and the others hit the city as it continued to rain Clovis.

On the other side of United States in New York City, there was a man that had been working all night. He was pasted out at his desk. The sun was coming up, and he had been in the office all night. His boss walked to his desk and saw him asleep. "Wake up" the boss man yelled.

Then man woke up in fear, the boss was yelling at him. "You know you have work, and that we are on a deadline! You need to get your head out of your ass and show me some RESULTS!" Then man stood up, and had a look of pure rage on his face. "I won't take this anymore" His boss looked at him with a cross eyed look on his face. "So now the little bag of shit has finally found his ball" the boss man yelled.

"Don't talk to me like that! I am sick and fucking tired of putting up with you! All you do is boss me and everyone around. I'm done being your bitch! I never get to see my wife and kids because I am always here! You can take this job and shove it right up your ass! Because from this day forward. I, James Richard is walking out and standing up for himself!" As he yelled at his now former boss.

As James stood up and was walking away from the place he use to work. Just before he got to the elevator, he yelled out. "I am my own man, and will not be treated as if I was trash. You may not understand you arrogant jackass. I have my dignity, my self-respect. I have my pride!"

As pressed the button on the elevator, he was suddenly in pain as he dropped to his knees. As James screamed in pain, a small piece of metal fell out of his head onto the floor. Like all the others, the metal was covered in blood. As the pain went away, just like before. The small piece of metal covered in blood lifted off of the floor and then flew way. The blood covered metal broke the window and was gone.

Meanwhile in Colorado, There was a military unit awaiting their flight for a deployment they were about to embark on. There was one of the companies that was waiting for their flight to board and taken off. Captain Fuiava, the company commander was waiting with his soldiers. When a group of four soldiers along with a man in a military dress uniform came walking up. The group of men walked right up to Captain Fuiava and spoke to him.

"Captain Fuiava, I'm General Blackwell. I have orders from our commander and chief to pick you and your company up time now, to be taken to Washington DC. The President of the United States has new orders for you and your men."

Captain Fuiava was in shock. "Roger sir, we are ready to leave." He replied to the four star general. Captain Fuiava then turned around facing his men and yelled out. "Company, we have new orders from our commander in chief, we will be leaving with General Blackwell now, so grab your bags!"

General Blackwell said to Fuiava, "Your transportation is ready for your men to load up." The company now made their way outside following the General Blackwell.

As the sun was rising up for the dawn of a new day, there was seven pieces of metal covered in blood all flying in the air. As the pieces of metal where flying in the air, the blood that was on all seven piece started to dry up. The seven pieces were all on the way to Las Vegas, Nevada. As the pieces flew into the city that early morning, passed right by main part of the city and all landed just on the outskirts of the Las Vegas. The pieces all hit the ground one by one and went into the dirt.

After all seven pieces could not be seen anymore, the ground started to rumble for a moment. The ground stopped, and just moments after the ground stopped moving. A skeleton hand came out of the ground. Soon more and more of the skeleton came out of the ground. Soon enough a full body skeleton was laying on the ground. The body of bones started to move, the bones started to crawl.

As the skeleton crawled, flesh started too grown on the bones. The body continued to crawl, more flesh grew on the bones. The body stopped and started to stand up slowly. The face now had eyes, and now skin started to grow over the flesh. As the body stood up, and skin had grown all over the body. Now there was a bald man with light skin, brown eyes, with an athletic body. Stood there with no clothes on with what looked to be a sinister smile on his face started walking right for the city.

TO BE CONTINUED...

BEHIND

THE

SCENES

MOMENTS

The following is not part of the Ying Yang story, but instead is a group of skits with characters from the Ying Yang Series. The skits you are about to read is just the author of the Ying Yang adding something. Extras for fans of series to have a good laugh with. For more on Ying Yang, please go visit

www.facebook.com/yingyangseries

www.facebook.com/leroyweedenjr

www.yingyang1.com
www.enchantmentlineproductions.com

BEHIND THE SCENES MOMENT: 001: "BED TIME"

April: "It's getting late. I'm going to bed."

Darkside: "It is getting late. I am going to sleep too. I felt like going to sleep an hour ago."

April: Didn't you just wake up from a nap an hour ago?

Darkside: Yeah, but a nap is a short time of sleep. Going to bed means long time of sleep.

Chaos: That's my brother, sleeps 20 hours a day and fights the bad guys Trinity's brother can't beat.

BEHIND THE SCENES MOMENT: 002: "GYM TIME"

Chaos: I miss the training from back home.

April: You can go to the gym here in the city and lift weight to get stronger.

Chaos: It won't work. I went a few days, and I had 6 of 45 pound plates on the bar and I did 5,000 reps. I still didn't feel like I was warmed up yet.

April: I forgot you guys are super strong. Maybe you could just sleep more? It seems to be working for Darkside.

Chaos: No, that's my brother being lazy.

Darkside: Hey! I need my rest. I don't have to take this, I'm gonna go take a nap!

BEHIND THE SCENES MOMENT: 003: "AT THE CLUB"

Chaos: This flavored water is great!

April: That's not flavored water, its whiskey.

Chaos: Whiskey huh? I'll take another one.

April: but you've already had 20 shots in the last 30 minutes.

Chaos: Your right, can't I just get a bottle of this stuff? These little glasses of shots goes way to fast.

April: A normal man would have been pasted out by now.

Chaos: Like my brother?

BEHIND THE SCENES MOMENT: 004: "IN THE LAB"

Stan: Now that the holiday season is over, we can continue on the plans.

Mark: Why did we wait till after the holidays to take over the world?

Stan: Well, I like to spend time with family and friends. I don't want are plans for taking over the world to be in the way.

Mark: Ok, so why didn't we start in January?

Stan: Well, I didn't want to start of the year to crazy. You know, so we are starting in February instead.

Mark: Well, I kinda wanted to spend time with my girlfriend for Valentine's Day.

Stan: Oh, well, we can put off the take over until the 15th.

Mark: That's great! I will be able to Jackie out, would kill me if I told her I couldn't and had to work.

Stan: Well, since, I am giving you the 14th off. You think you can see if I can take out Jackie's sister sometime? You know, put in a good word for me.

Mark: You want a girlfriend? Won't get in the way of your of your late nights at the lab?

Stan: It will, but I get so lonely sometimes. Plus I'm getting old, I'm 30 and still single.

Mark: Wow, I would have never guess you have a soft side.

Stan: What's that supposed to mean?

Mark: Nothing….. ("And all this time I was thinking he was cold heartless killer, he is a big softy deep down inside. Kinda funny, now I know he just puts on a façade to act like a big strong bad guy." Thinking to himself.)

Stan: What's up with that look on your face Mark?

Mark: What? No, nothing. No reason at all boss.

YINGYANG1.COM

173 | P a g e

www.ingramcontent.com/pod-product-compliance
Lightning Source LLC
Chambersburg PA
CBHW070924130626
46555CB00001B/269